First edition independently printed 2023.
This edition printed 2024 by Pope Lick Press.

DEREK HEATH

EMPIRE OF COLD

POPE LICK PRESS

2024

PART ONE

ONE

NORTH

The blades shuddered, no longer scything smoothly through the air but ripping it to pulpy shreds of viscera, as the helicopter lowered itself slowly to the ice. A blizzard of plump white projectiles batted the body of the vehicle, punching inches-thick glass and reinforced steel and fanning into a mist above the rotor. The Mi-8 chopper swayed as it descended, blue wedges of mountain swinging into view beyond vast planes of shining, crystalline nothing.

Oliver Cale gripped a battered metal pail between his legs, his head bowed low. Beneath the ragged fringe of his oilskin's woollen hood, thick tangles of long, brown hair fell into his eyes and mouth. His teeth were clamped together, his throat bobbing constantly as he swallowed down every dry-heave and surge of nausea.

"You're gonna miss this when we're out there in the cold!" Diana yelled over the pounding of the rotors.

She was perched across the cabin from him, her own hair billowing in knotted strands of sandy-gold. Her hood hung loosely around her shoulders, a bulky pair of headphones pressed tightly over her ears. The padded receiver of the headset's microphone hung suspended in front of her mouth, a blot of black attached to a rigid wire separating her cheek into parts.

"Not fucking likely!" Cale called back, glancing up briefly. Sharp grey eyes flared brightly through the tendrils of his hair, then lowered again as another ball of nausea swelled in his mouth and he tipped his head into the bowl. There was a dreadful wet groan and a splash; Diana was surprised he had anything left in his stomach to come up. She grinned, tightening her grip on a hanging canvas handhold and turning her head to look out of the window. Wide swathes of pink scalloped the horizon, banks of gold careening off the surface of the great glaring ball of the sun. The sky was bone-white and mirrored below by a tundra of pack ice, shallow dunes rolling into distant tables of miasmic blue; the falling snow punctuated everything with a swirling fog-like haze.

There could have been anything out there.

The landing skids of the helicopter clapped down on the snow and the helicopter jounced awfully, slamming Diana back into the wall of metal behind her. The canvas strap in her hand snapped taut and she yelped. A squawk of apologetic rambling detonated from the headphones as the pilot and co-pilot snapped at buttons and dials in the cockpit. The rotor blades continued slowing above them and the constant vibrating of the helicopter shell around them began to dull. They had smashed into the crust of the arctic and, after a few seconds, the Mi-8 started to settle. The churning blades seemed to just grow fatigued and give up, their movements winding down to nothing.

Over the banging of the cockpit doors and the yelling of the twin pilots, Diana finally heard the howling wind. In the absence of the whirring, chopping noise of the rotor blades, the shrill whistle-scream of the blizzard was apocalyptic.

"You good?" she called across the cabin. Strewn between her and Cale were a pair of stuffed duffel bags and a silver briefcase, clamped shut, filled with electronics. A bunch of other shit – presumably belonging to the pilots – rocked gently among their own possessions.

Cale thrust up a gloved thumb, keeping his head down.

Diana grimaced in the man's direction, the polite expression of friendliness disappearing from her face in an instant. She had met him at base camp and immediately taken a dislike to him. He was ex-military and carried himself like somebody itching for another tour, angry at everyone, teetering on the edge of violence. She had watched from a distance as he slammed his pack into the co-pilot's chest and told him – not asked him – to get it on board. Now there were flecks of vomit in the man's thick, dark beard. Evidently, he did not travel well.

The door thundered open suddenly and the helicopter rocked on its skids as a thick swell of wind punched into the cabin. A flurry of snow clumped on the floor and began to settle and Diana leaned to grab her bag as the pilot beckoned them outside. "Come on," she called, "you ready?"

"Always," Cale smiled thinly, raising his head. With the back of a gloved hand he wiped his mouth, then set down the bucket. When he stood he was tall enough that he had to bend his head to avoid bumping the cabin ceiling. Broad-shouldered and barrel-chested, he was a giant of a man. Diana hoped, bracing herself and moving to hop out of the helicopter, that there was more to discover about him than just his travel-sickness.

"Where are we?" she yelled over the wind as the pilot helped her down. Her boots crunched into the snow and she raised a hand to her eyes to shield them from the blinding sun. Beneath the top layer it felt as though the ground were hard, much harder than she had expected – almost like concrete or stone. "I thought you were going to take us right to the research station!"

The pilot's face was largely hidden behind the visor of a chunky helmet, his upper body swallowed by a blood-red coat that looked like it had been zippered at several different points. He gestured behind him as

Diana set her bag down in the snow and, behind her, Cale stepped blindly out of the cabin. The pilot was saying something as he waved vaguely into the white but his voice was lost in the wind and all Diana caught were unintelligible bursts of noise.

"What?" Cale yelled, stepping up behind her.

Diana jumped as a hand clapped down on her shoulder. Turning, she saw that the co-pilot had appeared behind them. With his hand still on her arm, he looked from Diana to Cale and pointed at the helicopter's landing skids. Diana frowned.

The helicopter was parked on a half-obscured square of what looked like grey slate, about six metres by six. In fact the three of them were standing on it. Concrete, smoothed down by the constant wind and snow. A perfectly flat landing pad, the edges obscured by shallow drifts, the aggregate surface a pale shade of used grey. They had touched down exactly where they were meant to.

Turning back to the pilot, Diana yelled, "I don't understand!"

Facing them both, the pilot staggered closer and said, as loudly as possible, "This *is* the research station!"

He beckoned again toward the endless tundra, the only landmarks for miles the crest of a steel-blue glacier on the horizon and, hardly visible at all, a pack of three or four polar bears migrating across the ice. Tiny white smears, that was all they were, through an unrelenting swirl of cotton wool.

Diana and Cale looked at each other. The tall man still had a little vomit in his beard, but this didn't satisfy her dislike for him as it had before; a deep, sickly unsteadiness had settled in her stomach. She swallowed. Looked out again at the empty snowscape.

The research building was gone.

Snow blew in her face as she walked out onto the tundra, the thick ice beneath that powdery crust creaking loudly beneath her. This was not her first time in the arctic but still she was wary of stepping too hard: the ice here could have been somewhere between three and six feet thick, even more perhaps, but there was always the chance that it would split open at her feet and she'd be sucked right into the freezing blue void of the Arctic Ocean. And if it felt cold up here…

"What are you looking for?" Cale called behind her. "Hey! There's nothing out here, love!"

Diana seethed, stumbling forward and raising both hands to draw her hood up over her head. "The fuck did you call me?" she muttered to herself, her voice swallowed by the billowing snow. All around them the sky was a vast upturned bowl of pink and yellow, the blinding sun pulsing thickly as it approached the knife-blade of the horizon at an impossibly slow pace. Elsewhere in the world the clawing hands of night dragged it below the ground at sunset; here, it pulled back. Resisted. It looked like night was coming, but she knew that it was still a way off. And when it came, it would stick around for a good six months.

Half a year of darkness.

Diana Clark couldn't help but wonder what the sunrise looked like.

"Christ, what—" she started as something tangled around her ankle. Looking down, she kicked at the thing and saw that she had stepped into a fluttering blanket of scrappy plastic mesh, the first sign of humanity since they'd started away from the helicopter. Glancing back over her shoulder, she yelled, "I found something!"

Cale was only a dozen feet behind her but his broad-shouldered silhouette was grey and blurry at the edges, beaten violently by the snow. Diana turned her attention away from the soldier as he approached, focusing on the ground around her. Stumbling forward a few steps, she saw further chunks of debris reveal themselves, most half-buried, scraps of mangled steel and ragged bricks of concrete poking out of the snow. Before she had taken another ten steps she was surrounded and wondered how she hadn't seen all of this before – looking back again, though, she realised that the helicopter had disappeared completely in the swirling white haze of the blizzard; they could only have walked half a mile at most. The arctic consumed everything, its screaming white mouth chewing silently and spitting out only fragments of miasmic colour.

Cale appeared suddenly out of the flurry and stood beside her, looking around at the carnage. His face was hard, jaw square and knotted with tension. His hood had been blown down and Diana was briefly distracted by the curls of a shadow crawling up the back of his skull. She caught a glimpse of black tendril, then the tall man tugged his hood up and the shape was gone. She caught his eye. "What d'you think happened here?"

"Oh, you want my opinion now?"

Diana frowned. "When did I say—"

Cale smiled thinly, his gaze returning to the debris. "I heard you talking to Ainsley before we came out here," he said. "I know *exactly* how you feel about me. You'd rather have another 'arctic expert' out here with you, right?"

"I'd rather not have a *soldier* out here with me," Diana said, swallowing, "but you don't need to take that personally. You should have said something before, I never meant—"

"You might've noticed, I was a little busy throwing up my last three breakfasts."

Diana hesitated. "Look, I'm sorry, I just – they asked me to come out here and find out what happened, and I don't know exactly what I can do – and I just think I'd be more confident if they'd sent another brain to help me figure this out, and not…"

The look in Cale's eyes sent a chill through her

unlike any cold she was feeling. Her gloved hands and her legs were numb, blood pumping weakly through the icy block of her chest like fragile beads of water through microscopic tunnels. That look made her feel like she was in a room with her father, and she felt as though that just might be the coldest place on Earth.

"I'm sorry," she said, "I'm not saying you're not… I'll be honest, it just scares me that you're here."

"I'm scaring you?" Cale said bitterly, cocking an eyebrow.

"Only because your presence implies a need for violence."

"You sound like my ex," Cale said. He winked, and Diana cringed as the shining point of his one open eye burrowed into her. She turned her eyes back to the wreckage of the research station. It was scattered all around, great slabs of stone thrust apart between knots of black metal and snow-spattered glass. One corrugated sheet of tin was planted firmly in the snow and the exposed half swayed dangerously in the wind, warping with every smack of snow.

"I don't know what the hell we're gonna tell them," Diana whispered.

The mayday had been short and desperate, a bundle of voices screaming through squawks of static. She had half-expected to find the place empty, dark. A couple of terrified scientists in a back room, huddling for warmth. They'd tell her a polar bear had broken in, or an angry huddle of arctic walrus; she'd help them back to the helicopter, and everything would be fine. Maybe a couple years' worth of work would be lost. That was just the way it went.

But there was no research station. Just a great snow-dusted crater in the pack ice where the tiny building had been ripped from its foundations, and a bundle of plastic mesh wrapped around her leg.

"We tell them they were right to send a soldier," Cale growled.

Diana looked up, squinting through a spray of gold-tinted snowfall into the distance. The tundra wasn't as flat as it first appeared, and she saw great standing icebergs on the horizon, white dunes rippling across the plain toward them. The dunes were scattered with hummocks and what looked like tiny cave entrances, and occasionally the tundra was punctuated with the peak of a rearing wedge of ice, miniature mountains forming massive teeth all around them.

"Come on," Cale said, spitting into the ice with a grimace. "We'd better give the place a quick scope before we give up on them."

Diana stared at him. "Give up on them? Christ, man, we're not going to—"

She was interrupted by a blast of sound behind them, the brief roar of the helicopter's engine followed by the whirring of the rotor blades, building and building until she could only imagine they were spinning at full speed. There was a sound like a yell, quickly silenced. Briefly she panicked, her eyes widening – were those bastards leaving them here? – but then the rotors slowed again and, after a minute or so, came to a stop. The only sound was the howling of the wind.

"Probably just keeping the engine warm," Cale shrugged. "Come on. Let's look around a bit."

Diana nodded. "Okay. But we're not just going to look for five minutes and give up. Those people are out here somewhere." *And they sounded fucking terrified,* she wanted to add, remembering the awful buzzing mania of the distress call. She had volunteered to come out and help with the search, but now she found herself wishing somebody else had answered the call. Guilt pulled at her stomach and she pointed. "I'll go this way."

"Fine," Cale said. He worked his jaw for a moment and Diana watched in disgust as he spat another gob of white at his feet.

"Jesus, stop that," she snapped. "Come on, help me out here."

"What are you, my mother?"

"Don't be a fucking child. Help me."

"Sure thing, ma'am—"

He stopped suddenly and Diana blinked, the arctic wind batting at her chest and stomach as she waited for him to finish. But his teeth had clamped together and his eyes were locked hard on something behind her shoulder, and after a few moments she realised he wasn't planning on saying anything further. Dread crept through her body and she turned her head to look in the same direction.

There was a shape in the snow.

At first it was little more than a tiny smudge of black in the whirling miasma, but as she watched it began to grow. It moved like it was walking on two legs and momentarily Diana's heart was flooded with relief; the research station might have been wrenched from the ground, but the occupants had survived—

"What the…" she murmured as the shape approached. When it became too big to be a man she thought she might be watching an approaching musk ox or some kind of arctic moose, but the way the big grey shape moved was clearly human, or human-like at least…

"Big guy," Cale said quietly.

The man walked slowly, his legs thick as trunks. His shape was still largely indiscernible but Diana caught the flash of a red coat, the shape of a hood fluttering around his head. His hands hung at his sides as he moved. He was enormous. Oliver Cale was a good few inches taller than Diana, making him perhaps six-three or -four, but the figure approaching through the snow was taller still. Seven feet tall. Eight, maybe. No, that was ridiculous. Still…

The titanic figure had stopped moving and it stood perhaps a quarter-mile from them, its face obscured by the snow. It seemed to vibrate as the blizzard pinwheeled around it, the pink smear of the sky behind its head forming a scalloped halo of colour.

For a full minute, the colossus watched them. She couldn't see its eyes, but she knew that it was watching.

Then it started to move again.

TWO

WHITE, WHITE, AND RED ALL OVER

"I think we should go back to the helicopter."

Cale wasn't listening to her. His eyes were fixed on the figure walking toward them. It seemed to bulge and blur in the snow, built like a wrestler and faceless in the haze of white that sliced through it. His heart was racing, not yet pounding but fluttering as if the connecting wires that kept it suspended in his chest were trying to snap it back and forth. Images flashed relentlessly across his mind: the snow became a bloom of dust and gunsmoke, the approaching figure three or four shapes moving hurriedly through the blood and the sand; his breathing had stopped, no, it was going too fast, he was sucking at the bitterly cold air while the heat of that memory burned his face—

"Cale," Diana said, clamping a hand on his arm. "We should go."

The memory imploded, leaving him staring at the

oncoming giant of a man. The figure in the red coat must have been seven-foot seven. Seven-foot eight, maybe. Wide, too, chest like a steamroller. Cale's breathing had slowed and he wondered briefly if Diana had seen him go to that awful dark room or if she'd been watching the man too. Didn't matter.

"Now," she said, and he nodded.

As he started to back away, Cale caught a flash of white on the figure's massive face. Were those teeth? He turned, following Dana into the snow in what he hoped was the direction of the helicopter.

"Hurry up," Diana called, and he grunted a reply.

Glancing over his shoulder, he scoured the snow for any sign of the figure, but the enormous man had gone. The mountainous shape had disappeared into the snow; had they somehow gone out of range? Had he ever been there at all? It was impossibly cold and Cale had on more than one occasion been forced to see things in front of him that weren't really there. But this felt different. He stopped looking back and walked faster, boots crunching in the snow.

Diana had frozen still.

He looked around as he reached her. Ahead of them the dull silhouette of the Mi-8 had appeared in the blizzard, its edges blurry and vague but the shape mostly recognisable. It was still twenty or thirty yards away. "What is it?" he said.

"Look down."

He did. "What the fuck…"

Red paint had spattered the snow at their feet in a slimy curve, tiny spots and softly-spreading pools forming a blotchy, crimson smile. The paint steamed gently into the air, blossoms of vapour rising off each semi-congealed print. Cale had almost stepped in the stuff. Beside him Diana stepped gingerly across the line and walked a few steps farther before turning her head. "There's more…"

Cautiously, Cale followed.

The first fan of steaming red slop was followed by another, a few feet closer to the helicopter. This wicked grin of red was thicker, wetter, and the steam that rose from each glob made it a good six inches into the air before being hammered into nothing by the snow. Looking left and right, Cale saw that he wasn't looking at a painted smile at all: the grinning red mouth continued in both directions, curving around to form a smeared circle. The spatter was frantic and angular, every thread of paint tipped off to the side as though somebody had stood in the very centre of the ring with a can and wheeled around on the spot as they slopped it out into the snow.

"Christ," he whispered, looking up. A few more feet and there was another circle, this one even thicker and darker. And here the concentric rings became less defined and more conjoined, melting into one another, overlapping—

Cale was running before he could stop to think, hurtling toward the hazy shadow of the helicopter. His boots smashed into the snow and blood and he found himself lurching into a central circle of red pools that were so thick and hot the steam blooming from them was like bonfire smoke. The inner circle was so mad and wild and bright against the white that he thought, for a second, he'd finally gone mad.

Beside him, Diana said something. He didn't hear her. He was busy staring up at the helicopter.

The rotor blades of the Mi-8 were drooling, thick red ropes of blood peeling off the edges like threads of skin pulled from the top of a bowl of gravy that had been sitting around for too long. The gluey strings dripped dreadfully into the snow, the blades themselves coated so thickly that he couldn't remember them ever being a colour *other* than red. The steel body of the chopper had been splashed with blood and the windows were punctuated with thick, dribbling runnels of the stuff. Briefly Cale remembered hearing the blades warm up, spin at full speed, then shudder to a stop again, and there again was that image: some idiot artist pivoting on the spot with a one-point-five-gallon paint can in his arms, throwing ribbons of it into the snow—

"The pilot," Diana whispered, and her voice cut through the snow.

Chunks of meat and bone had sprayed the snow around them but, heavier than the blood, had sunk into the crust so that they were half-buried and more difficult to discern through the flurry. Barely a yard from where Cale stood, the pilot's arm poked up out of the tundra. The ragged stump was still bleeding beneath the snow, though the cold seemed to have stemmed the flow somewhat; the blood that pooled around it was an ugly purple. The fingers might have been curled into claws, but they had been sliced off as the arm was flung from the rotor blades; a clean diagonal cut had lopped off the entirety of the pinky finger, most of the middle and ring, and the tip of the index. The points of bone sticking out of the stumps were smeared with greasy red. Nearer to the helicopter, a shipwreck of ribcage and deflated lung stood upturned on the concrete landing pad, spattered with clear, gristly chunks of intestine.

The rest of him was nowhere to be seen.

"Where's the other guy?" Cale said quietly, but before Diana could attempt a reply he had answered his own question. His eyes locked onto the Mi-8's cockpit and his teeth locked together, his head pounding. Later, he would remind himself that he had seen worse in the Helmand Province. But right now his entire body was locked up, no longer shuddering with the cold but solid and lead-like. Useless, frozen to the spot.

The cockpit door was open. It swung in the wind, gluey ropes of red running down the inside, spattered dots coating the outside. The co-pilot was sat in his seat, body turned toward the open door so that he could look out at them. His head was tipped back, eyes wide and round in a face splashed with blood. His mouth was open and his tongue had been wrenched forward so that it lay bulging like some ruptured fruit on his lower teeth.

His stomach had been ripped open. His intestines were coiled in his lap, still twitching – though not with the same jerkiness they would have been had the cold not subdued them significantly – and the cavity of his gut was a ragged black hole. The organs below his feet had frozen already and steam discharged from his exposed insides in a thick, white plume.

"What the hell do we do?" Diana said, suddenly right behind him.

"I don't know," Cale said, dread flooding his veins. "Christ, I don't… we have to get out of here."

"How? They're dead," Diana said desperately, "they're both—"

A shadow lurched over them both, blotting out the blinding white sunlight. The soaked-metal smell of frozen blood and oil was replaced by the thick, fruity stench of ripe meat and Cale looked up, already knowing what he'd see.

The eight-foot man in the red coat and hood loomed over them, grinning with enormous, white teeth. Shark's teeth, flaring with snowlight.

Diana screamed.

The titanic figure was haloed by a blinding surge of sunlight but, in the sharp half-second before the world exploded around her, Diana saw his face for the first time. Her eyes widened and she shrieked in terror as the man loomed over them, his eyes flashing hungrily.

He must have been eight and a half feet tall, much bigger than she'd originally thought. His body was packed into padded polar clothing, the combat trousers and thick red oilskin billowing around his colossal frame as the wind batted uselessly at him. His boots must have been a size twenty, the laces a bright blood-red, the leather worn and greasy. His hood was pulled up and the woolly fringe whipped about his face, the ragged tassels tossed amongst threads of thick, grey hair. His jaw was square and bulging knots of muscle seemed to be trapped in his cheeks; his lips were thin, pulled back from purple gums and massive tombstone teeth. The sound was lost in a whirlwind of snow, but she could tell he was laughing.

"What do you—"

Cale was thrown back into the ice as a fist the size of a bowling ball smashed into his throat. Diana's scream died in her throat and she clamped a hand over her mouth, taking a staggering step back from the giant. His head turned toward her and she saw that he had stopped grinning, his lips firmly pressed together. Thick chips of ice-white stubble punctuated the sinuous flesh of his jaws and the top of a neck that seemed to be formed entirely of thick cables of muscle. His forehead and nose were scarred, ribbons of soft white tissue crisscrossing the skin like veins. The flesh itself was flaking and grey in places, like chalk or stone. His left cheek and a ring around the left eye were riddled with sores.

His eyes burned like the sun.

"We don't want any trouble," Diana called into the blizzard, taking another step back as she raised both her hands in surrender. Behind her she heard Cale gasping for breath, sucking at the air and scrabbling onto his knees. White smears streaked his clothes where he had fallen, beads of half-melted snow scattering his hair like tiny shards of glass. "Whoever you are, we just want to go—"

The word *home* was squeezed out of her throat in a hoarse whisper as the gargantuan man lunged forward and grabbed her neck with one hand. Before she could try and bat him away she felt her body lift into the air and gasped, reaching up to grab his arm. Her hands curled uselessly around the man's fingers and her legs kicked beneath her, two feet above the snowy crust. The intensity of the white-whirling storm around her seemed to have been dialled up to twelve and she could hardly see, black clouds of fog creeping into the edges of her vision. The man's palm was like stone, his thick fingers crushing the air out of her windpipe. Her body swung as she kicked and swiped at him but her head was throbbing, blood in her ears, the sharp white points of his eyes threading into her through the snow. He was going to kill her.

"Hey!" Cale yelled somewhere in the distance.

Diana's eyes rolled up into her skull as her lungs clawed desperately at the vestiges of air in her throat. He sounded like he was miles away. "Eat this, pig-fuck!"

She saw a blur of green and felt the man's grip loosen around her neck. Air swelled into her chest as she inhaled desperately; the giant let her go, punching his entire bodyweight into the attacking soldier before she had even hit the ground. He was big. And fast. Jesus Christ, what the hell *was* this thing?

Cale yelled as the man punched a stony fist into his shoulder. There was an awful, wet *crack!* and the soldier stumbled back, crumpling to his knees. There was a glint of bright rage and Diana knew that the colossus was looking at her again, heaved herself to her feet and staggered back. They had to get away, to—

A boulder-like knee crashed up into her diaphragm and she was blown backward, turning head over heels and barrelling into the crust. The snow was searing against the side of her face and in her mouth. Her ribs felt like a bundle of blunt knives pressed into her lungs; winded and agonised, she tipped back her head to look up, staring through a snapping tangle of damp hair as the giant reached down and grabbed Cale by the arm. She heard yelling, watched helplessly through spangles of throbbing light as the soldier was tossed toward the helicopter like a ragdoll.

"Leave him alone!" she yelled hoarsely, trying to get to her feet. A dozen feet from her, the giant hauled

Cale off the ground with one hand and wrenched open the helicopter's cabin door with another. Diana screamed as Cale was shoved into the cabin, his body somehow limp and rigid all at once. "Hey! Leave him the fuck alone!"

The titan turned around, grinning again. His eyes blazed, tombstone teeth flashing with cruel virility.

"Leave him…"

Diana's eyes went wide again as the man lurched toward her, crossing the distance in two powerful strides and launching a fist toward her face. She ducked the first, almost falling into the snow again as the giant's knuckles whistled through the air above her head. She wasn't quick enough for the second; from somewhere off to the side – left or right, didn't matter – a violent hook caught her in the nose, ripping a deep hot stripe of pain across her face. Diana yelled and pinwheeled, falling onto her face in the snow. Blood misted her eyes and she screamed in pain as thick fingers twisted into her hair and wrenched her head upward. Red strings connected her broken nose to the snowy crust for a second and then snapped, the blood already freezing. She was whipped onto her back and stared up through a haze of crimson as the big man reached down with both hands and grabbed her by the armpits, throwing her easily over his shoulder. The world swung on a blood-sprayed pendulum and her brain smashed into the inside of the skull. As easily as if she were a bag of potatoes, the giant heaved her toward the helicopter and flung her body into the cabin.

With an awful *crunch* she smacked into the wall and flopped down it, ears pounding as runnels of blood streaked across her face. She looked up to see the cabin door slamming shut and then the helicopter turned on its side and she screamed as she and Cale were thrown against the ceiling. Somewhere at the very edge of her vision she registered a curtain of snow spraying across the window. The co-pilot's body tumbled in a slow circle in the cockpit and landed on the controls.

Through his goggling, rheumy eyes, the dead man watched Diana howl in agony as the titanic beast of a man clamped his hands around the Mi-8's tail and steadily, impossibly – with a grating, scraping sound like two tectonic plates grinding together – started to drag the eleven-tonne helicopter across the tundra.

THREE

NEST

Diana Clark's dreams were murky and punctuated by throbbing ribbons of pain, any sense of hazy stillness denuded from her by a deep, rhythmic thumping far beneath her body. It was the movement of the world: the cosmic shifting of leagues of water rolling on the ragged undersides of icy plateaus, the back-and-forth of the ocean. *Thwum. Thwum. Thwum—*

Her eyes snapped open, a blistered film of dried blood cracking apart. A little ran into her left eye and she winced, blinking rapidly as she eased herself into a sitting position. Her head pounded and she raised a hand to her temple, massaging with the heel of her palm. "Ugh," she moaned, forcing her eyes open wide and peering through the clouds of black stars that had appeared and danced before her. "Where…"

The room came into her field of vision all at once, swinging left-to-right before finally, blindingly blasting itself into view. She was surprised to see that she was no longer in the helicopter; in those last few seconds before she'd passed out, she had thought that it – it, and the swooping bank of snow outside the windows – might just be the last thing she ever saw.

She was intensely cold and grabbed the folds of her coat, pulling them tight across her chest and hugging her body tightly. Glancing furtively about she saw that she was in a small room, about the width of the Mi-8's interior and perhaps twice as long. She had been slumped against the back wall and across from her was a steel bulkhead door with a colossal wheel hammered into its body. Beside her was a small pair of bunks and scattered across the floor was a mess of damp rags and shattered equipment. The blankets were gone, though one was bunched around her waist; it seemed somebody had wrapped it around her as she slept and it had fallen away in her fitful twitching. She grabbed it, covering her shoulders, and rubbed her hands together as she stood. The ground was tipped to one side and the unsteadiness that rocked her body was incredible and overwhelming. Falling back against the wall, she closed her eyes and took a breath.

"Where the hell am I?" she murmured, darkness clouding her vision as she turned her head to face the door again. Suddenly panicking she lurched across the room, crashing through foggy blooms of her own breath. The walls seemed to close in and something glassy crunched under her boot as she stamped forward, moving clumsily, heart pounding.

She half-expected the door to be locked. She grabbed the wheel with both hands and hissed as the cold metal seared her palms, even through the thick material of her gloves. It span loosely as she propelled it counter-clockwise – almost too loosely, and for a moment she was terrified that the lock had been broken and the wheel wasn't connected to anything – then there was a booming *clunk* and the door swung open, almost tipping her forward. Blood drizzling into her mouth from a split in the congealed red cake on her cheek, she stumbled forward into a miasma of flickering electric light. Pulses of colour smashed into her and she swung her body into the nearest wall, batting away a vaguely arm-shaped thing as it reached up to her from somewhere near the floor.

"Where… out," she muttered, "can't keep me here—"

Somewhere in the back of her head, she registered faintly that she was inside the research station. She had emerged from a small cabin into a somewhat larger room, the edges bulging with angular countertops and cupboards. Somewhere to the right a three-bar heater throbbed weakly into the brittle air, tiny spouts of warmth detonating into nothing before they could reach the centre of the room. Dark shapes sat around her in a circle, half a dozen of them perhaps, but she could only see the vague pink blobs of their faces through the haze of agony wracking her body. Somebody was saying something. Didn't matter. Out.

Out.

A door at the opposite end of the room. She staggered drunkenly for it, almost tripping on an outstretched leg which was quickly whipped back to let her past. Her boots were soaked and felt like they were full of lead; her whole body swayed as she moved.

"Out..."

She hammered her body into the door and spun the wheel. There was more resistance to this one and she had to scramble to shunt the mechanism across its rollers, ignoring the shouting behind her and the thick wet thumping in her chest, ignoring the

Thwum. Thwum. Thwum.

below her feet. She had seen the blueprints of the research station before they'd come and knew that beyond this door there was a short entrance corridor and a small kitchen. At the far end of the corridor was the final bulkhead door, and beyond that, the outside world—

The door swung open and she fell through, tumbling to her knees and howling at the immediate blast of frozen air. The door slammed behind her with a titanic boom and she stumbled to her feet, squinting through a funnel of swirling wind into the sweeping, curving wall of arctic blue before her.

The outside world.

Wheeling around and clamping her arms across her chest, she stumbled back and looked up in terror at the research station. The front of the building had been ripped violently away, leaving a halo of mangled metal and concrete around the bulkhead door through which she had collapsed. The building – what little was left of it, at least – keened to one side, half-buried in the snow, orange piping forming garish runnels through the concrete. The edge of the roof had curled back where the segments had been wrenched apart, and a fringe of bent steel glinted with great fat stripes of greasy light.

She was shivering but her body felt still. Since she had woken up time seemed to have been rushing backward past her but now it slowed to its usual pace, then slowed further. Stopped.

She looked around.

The walls of the enormous cavern were a smooth, glassy blue, arches of spangly light funnelled into each slope so that the great open space was like the inside of some crystalline cathedral. There were great trenches in the cave floor where the research station had been dragged through the ice, and where the surviving half of the building had been dumped, drifts of snow had formed lilting mounds and ramps against what had once been its south wall. Above it, thick spiralling icicles hung from the curl of a sky-blue dome which bubbled and blistered into the ceiling of the cave, half a mile or so above her head.

Taking shuddering steps back, Diana swung her head around to look about the rest of the cavern. Her crunching steps echoed in the awful quiet, tendrils of wind barrelling through faraway tunnels and whistling softly into the cave the only other sound. The walls shone with beads of sunlight bleeding through layers and layers of centuries-old ice, the immense ceiling a labyrinth of glacially-dripping spines and concave white panels. She couldn't see a way out but knew that there must be one, however distant, for the ice beneath her was blown with a thick layer of snow and here and there more drifts had gathered against the walls. Off to her left, almost completely obscured by more snow, was the rest of the research station: it lay in bent pieces, each twisted around another, doors and sections of wall scattered like some child's abandoned building bricks in the ice and covered with a patina of frost. To her right and a little behind her, an overturned snowmobile had been thrown against the far wall, the skis strangled by coils of frozen rubber track, the back of the machine a mess of sprockets and crumpled metal. The glass windshield was shattered.

Slowly she walked into the middle of the space, her eyes locked on a vast swathe of blackness that swallowed half of the cavern: a gargantuan, solid thing nosed halfway in, sixty feet high and spreading backward from the black knife of its head to a curved beam almost twice as vast.

The N.S. *Yazychnik* had crashed into the cavern, a nuclear icebreaker tipped to port and looming impossibly high above her. Its shadow was fluid and swelled across the roof of the broken research station, huge explosions of snow and ice forming spires of destruction at its bow. The ship was immense. Diana couldn't see onto the deck but a number of cargo containers had fallen into the cave and formed a crude staircase of corrugated iron up the walls of the giant ice structure. The icebreaker creaked ominously.

Diana swallowed.

The door closed behind her, the airtight seal clamping loudly into place. Bright purple shapes sprayed her eyes, temporarily semi-blinded by the bright crystal walls of the cave. As they faded she looked around the room, her teeth gritted together, her heart finally slowing. It had been a small common area when the research station was intact; now, it had been turned into some kind of all-purpose hub. A wide swathe of the far counter was scattered with knives and empty food packs; beside these, a translucent plastic bag had been filled with fish scales and skins and tied loosely. She could smell them nonetheless. The heater stood in the centre of the room, a thick cable leading to the wall. Now that the drumming in her ears had subsided she could hear the distant humming of a struggling generator. Six pairs of eyes watched her from the edges of the room, six shivering bodies wrapped in sleeping bags and blankets and huddled close together.

"Hi," she whispered.

From the corner closest to her, Oliver Cale looked up and nodded gently. He sat with his hands dangling between his knees, a thick wool blanket tossed across his shoulders. Still, she could see that his left arm was all out of whack, probably dislocated; his arm hung at an odd angle, the fingers throbbing and red. He had removed his gloves and she saw that they were slowly drying on the floor beside the three-bar heater. "You good?" he said quietly.

She looked from Cale to the others and nodded. "I'm good. Sorry, I... I panicked. What the hell is going on?"

The others looked at each other. Evidently nobody wanted to be the one to tell her what had happened or where they were; the uncomfortable silence told her they had already had this conversation a couple times.

Eventually one of the others spoke up, a woman who looked to be in her mid-forties. She sat against the opposite wall, her coat zipped up to her neck, her grey hair unwashed and yellowing. "You saw him," she said, her voice hoarse and weak. Her eyes were denuded of colour. "I'm sure you can figure it out."

"Him?" Diana turned to Cale, her eyes briefly meeting those of a tall, narrow-bodied Black man as her head swept to the left. "Okay. What *is* he?"

Cale shook his head, his eyes darkening.

The grey-haired woman cleared her throat, drawing Diana's attention back across the room. She was dressed in some kind of naval uniform, Diana realised, the collar stiff and blue beneath the coat. The coat itself was too big to be hers. Six of them now, including Cale – seven, including herself – so how many had died out here? How many had that man – that *thing* – killed?

"We call him Goliath," said the grey-haired woman.

"Big fucker," Cale whispered.

"Big fucker," the woman agreed. "Scary fucker. The arctic belongs to him, I think. He spends half his time out there, hunting. Half his time in here."

"In here?"

"Not the research base," the woman shook her head. "He leaves us alone, mostly. Only comes in when… well. When he gets hungry. But the cave… that's his house."

"More than a cave," said the tall Black man to Diana's left, and she turned to look at him. His face was serious, his eyes a deep earthy brown. His head was shaved and his left ear pierced with a single silver stud; between the folds of a blanket pulled around his chest, she saw a silver of the same uniform. "This place is a labyrinth."

"You two came from the icebreaker," Diana realised. "Is that right?"

The Black man nodded. "Ice navigator," he said, pointing grimly up at his chest with a gloved hand. "Dean Kirton."

"And you?"

"Captain Shaw," the grey-haired woman said. "We're all that's left."

Diana looked to the right. Three others sat huddled together, a sleeping bag spread across the wall behind them and another laid across their laps. A blonde woman sat with a mug in her hand and what looked like some half-eaten pinkish scraps of flesh inside. Beside her, a scrawny man with eyeglasses and a mess of thatched black stubble had his eyes on the floor; a young Korean woman leant her head on his shoulder. She had been crying. "You three?" Diana said.

"We were in the building when he ripped it out of the ground," the blonde woman said quietly, looking up from her mug. It was fish, Diana saw. Still violently pink and threaded with bones; it had only been half-cooked. "I was checking out the core samples. I don't… I don't really know what happened next."

"There were twelve of you," Diana whispered. "Did any—"

"No," said the bearded man. He pushed his glasses up his nose. The left lens was mashed into a network of frosty splinters. When he spoke again, she noted a thick Belfast accent: "No, they didn't."

"I'm Megan," the blonde woman said. "This is Henry. And Jae."

Diana nodded slowly. "Okay. Okay. So… three of you from the research station, two from the icebreaker. Anyone else?"

"Only Abel," the icebreaker captain said, raising a gloved hand to tuck a loose bank of grey, thin hair behind her ear. "Out the back."

"Out the back?"

"Fishing. He's always out there."

"Right. So, if I'm getting this straight, the big guy – Goliath – dragged your ship into this cave and planted a whole building in here too. How is that possible?"

"He's not human," Jae whispered. It was the first time she'd spoken and Diana glanced in her direction to see that her eyes were wide and wet with fear. Her hair, black and thick, was matted with blood. "He can't be…"

"He looks human," Diana said.

"For now," said the Black man. Dean, that was his name.

"What?"

Dean grinned. "*Soucouyant*," he whispered.

"I don't—"

"Shape-changer," he offered. "They look like us in the day. Traditionally, like withered old women. At night, they take off their skin and come for your blood."

"Don't be stupid," Henry spat bitterly across the room. "We've had enough of your folk stories."

"Okay," Diana said, raising her hands before the two could start arguing. "You said 'at night'. You understand night-time out here lasts for six months?"

Dean shrugged. "I'm aware. I'm also aware he doesn't look like a withered old woman. I'm just saying—"

"The sun is setting," Cale said.

"He's a man," Diana said firmly. "Big man, I know. And maybe there's something else there. But whatever the case—"

"If night is coming," the blonde woman – Megan – said, "then we're all in trouble. Shapeshifter or not."

"Why d'you say that?" Henry said quietly.

Megan's eyes locked onto Diana's. Her lips were tight. "We've been here for weeks now. the icebreaker"—here she looked in Captain Shaw's direction—"were here before us."

"A month, now," Shaw nodded.

"There were more of us," Megan continued. "He took them away. We don't know where… we think he eats them. Dozens."

"You're afraid he's coming for the rest of us," Diana said.

Megan frowned a little. "No," she said weakly. "I'm afraid hunting season's wrapping up. I'm afraid he's about to come into his nest and hibernate for the rest of the year. I'm afraid… I'm afraid we're his reserves."

"I don't understand."

"She's afraid," Cale said, "that the big bad monster's about to have a nice, long nap. And that whenever he wakes up, a little woozy, and fancies a midnight snack…"

"So we escape," Diana said, stepping into the middle of the room. "Right? It would be better to take the risk and try and get out of here, wouldn't it? Better than sitting around and waiting to—"

"Except we don't know the way out," Shaw said.

Jae shook her head. "He moves too quietly. Somehow. We don't ever know if he's coming or going until the door opens and he… and he…"

Henry wrapped an arm tightly around the young Korean woman and planted a soft kiss on her forehead. "It's okay. It's okay."

"We've got no choice," Shaw said. "We either go out there, and die…"

"Or wait here," Diana finished grimly, "and die."

FOUR

A BETTER PLACE

The arctic sky bristled with traces of something fantastic, whorls of green fluttering into existence only to be beaten away by the wind before they could clarify fully. Snow streamed in great tendrils, furrowing the edge of the icefield.

The ocean bellowed softly against the ice, a wall of deep green-grey curling over and over itself, occasional lashings of glassy foam freezing as they skittered onto the crust. A walrus lazed at the edge, lying on its side, great tusks glistening wetly. Its fur was like soaked velvet, a patina of frost crystals forming white patches across its body. Thin whiskers twitched as it sniffed the salty air, slowly batting a single fin against its belly.

The ice shuddered.

The walrus tipped up its head lackadaisically, looking up into the wind. Squinting, it crowed loudly, glanced almost furtively around, then lowered its head again. Flapping its tail once, the beast thumped a fan of crisp white into the crust beneath it.

Another footstep.

The walrus strained its neck to look up, bleating again. At first it saw nothing; just as the animal was about to lower its head again, however, it noted a smudge of grey in the distance. It held its position, gazing at the approaching figure. Growing.

Growing fast.

The walrus rolled onto its front, eyelids clamping together as it peered through the snow.

The figure was tall, broad-shouldered, wearing people clothes. But it wasn't people. Its left eye glinted in the fading sunlight, a tiny point of yellow in its face.

Closer.

Closer…

Fear turned in the walrus' stomach and it backed up, slipping toward the water's edge. A spray of cold ocean decorated its back as it pressed its head down, baring its tusks. The figure was running now. Red coat. Grey hands. Its face was… wrong…

The walrus bellowed as the tall man thundered toward it, and when the approaching figure didn't slow down the beast started to turn. Ice dragged beneath its belly as it heaved itself in a wide, flapping circle. It had to get in the water—

Before it could turn all the way around, a great grey fist ploughed into its back.

The walrus screamed, warmth spurting into the

snow. Tipping its head back, it spread its jaws wide, preparing to clamp its tusks down on the attacker's flesh. Its eyes widened as the massive man in the people clothes bore down on it, baring impossibly sharp teeth, grinning like the ocean.

There was a sound like tearing paper as the man punched his jaws into the animal's spine and ripped, ropes of viscera slopping onto the ice and steaming. The walrus shrieked, something awfully human about the sound.

It didn't carry very far. The wind swallowed the scream before it could reach anything that would listen.

Time was broken.

There was no way of knowing what the hour might have been when the two of them were shown to their temporary quarters – the small bunk in which Diana had woken up what felt like an eternity before – but it felt like midnight. It was impossible to tell from inside the research station, and even out in the cave the light was still the same; the sun was certainly setting, but infinitely slowly, and the spangles of blue were much the same ghastly temper that they had been before. Hours might have passed, but those hours felt simultaneously like they should have been minutes and like they had stretched into days. The only indicator that 'night' had fallen was the exhaustion. And Diana was *exhausted.*

Cale took the lower bunk, perching on the edge of it and lowering his hood. With both hands he reached up to remove the tangled hair from his face and then sat, for minutes, with his head in his hands. He had said very little since Diana had woken up. But in those brief moments where she caught his eye, she saw something that frightened her deeply: a lifeless kind of resignation. The soldier had given up.

Wearily Diana unfolded a plastic chair that had been stood by the door and sat on it, leaning her head against the wall behind her. She felt more than anything like crawling up into the top bunk and knew that she was tired enough to fall asleep quite easily, but worried that she might dream. That she would see *him* again. The heat from the three-bar hardly reached them in here, but the tightness of the room meant that at least their meagre body heat was dispersed thickly. The generator sounded weak and sickly.

She wondered if they would freeze to death before they starved.

Or perhaps they would be picked off before then. What if they *weren't* reserve stock for the enormous man's 'hibernation'? What if the eight of them were some final meal upon which Goliath would gorge himself before the six-month-long night set in?

What if she was next?

"Why did they come here?" she said aloud, hardly aware that her thoughts had slipped out of her mouth.

It was almost a minute before Cale looked up. When he did, she saw it again: the wet, splitting hopelessness in his eyes. "Who?"

"The icebreaker. Shaw. Dean," Diana said. "That's a big ship. Looked like they were doing a cargo run. D'you reckon they were bringing supplies to base camp? Surely we would have heard when we were back there – somebody would have said—"

"I don't know," Cale said flatly.

"We should ask them."

"Why?"

"Because it doesn't make sense. A Russian icebreaker with a deck full of cargo containers. That's a lot of supplies. Too many for the research station, and base camp would have said. So who were they supplying—"

"I don't know," Cale echoed. He turned, adjusting himself into a foetal position on the bunk. "And I don't care, love."

"Great," Diana snapped, glaring at him. "What's your problem?"

Cale said nothing.

"Come on. Grow up a little, would you? We can't just give up on them—"

"That lot?" Cale said bitterly. "We're as fucked as they are."

"'That lot' are scared," Diana said, "and we came to help them. Didn't we?"

"That was before."

"Before what?"

"Before we knew Ron Perlman's big brother had taken a bunch of steroids and claimed the arctic for his personal killing floor," Cale muttered. He turned over, glaring at her with narrowed eyes. "He dragged our helicopter across the ice, Diana. For miles. Nearly broke my fucking arm; I had to get… fucking… *whatshername* to relocate the fucking thing. He pulled an *icebreaker* into his nest, love, we're not… we're not getting out of here. Neither are they. End of."

"You don't know any of their names, do you?"

Cale raised an eyebrow. "What?"

"*That lot*," Diana said.

"Sure. Captain Mopey—"

"—Shaw—"

"—and the big bald guy who still believes in ghosts—"

"—*Dean*—"

"—and the other three."

"The other three?" Diana said, incredulous.

"Yeah. Blondie, Beardy, and… Cringer." He grinned, as if proud of himself. "You know, from *He-Man*?"

"Megan, Henry, and Jae. And the guy outside?"

"There's a guy outside?"

"For Christ's sake, Cale. He's been out there the whole time we've been here. As far as I know, he's the only one of us capable of getting hold of any kind of food out here."

"Ah. He would be the one responsible for the raw fish, then."

"D'you see any other options out here?" Diana spat. "Tell me his name."

"No."

"Tell me his fucking name."

"I don't know it!" Cale hissed. "Leave me the fuck alone, love!"

"It's Abel," Diana whispered.

"Fan-fucking-tastic."

"We're here to—"

"Save them," Cale said. "I know. But there's nothing we can do. Now shut the fuck up and let me sleep, would you?"

"Why? You got a big day planned tomorrow?"

"Oh, yeah. I'm gonna really get to know all the people I'm gonna *die* with."

"Shut up."

"You shut up."

"Cunt," Diana whispered under her breath.

Smiling thinly, Cale turned away again and pulled up his hood.

For a while Diana sat silently, her arms folded across her chest, boots planted firmly on the floor. The concrete rumbled softly beneath her and after a minute or two she found herself attuning the rhythm of her breathing to that deep, swelling beating deep beneath the ice:

Thwum.

Thwum.

Thwum…

After ten minutes she looked in Cale's direction. His chest rose and fell slowly, the hair in his face billowing softly as his own breaths punctuated the air around his mouth with wisps of vapour. She felt a swell of guilt; he was exhausted too, had been through the same ordeal and potentially come out of it worse… still, that didn't mean he wasn't an utter dick.

Diana closed her eyes and lowered her head. Palms laid flat on her knees, a patina of sweat gluing her hands to her gloves despite the cold, she let her hair fall loosely in front of her eyes and prayed.

I know there's every chance you're not listening, she thought, drawing in a deep breath. It was like inhaling glass. *I know I…*

Her thoughts were loose. Jumbled. What did she know?

I know I've been away for a while.

Anger flared in her stomach. A deep hatred that she struggled, at times like these, to keep buried.

I'm sure you can understand why.

Anyway…

"Oh, what's the point?" she whispered, eyes snapping open. Furtively she glanced toward Cale to make sure he hadn't heard anything. He still seemed to be asleep. Diana flexed her fingers. Tried not to think. Tried not to remember…

The images that flashed in front of her face were not

the usual stale negatives of her father. She saw vibrant pulses of red splashing the cream of white, saw Goliath grabbing the helicopter by the tail and wrenching it through the snow, carving a trench as she screamed.

She saw blood in a vast circle, fanned out by the rotor blades. Saw the co-pilot's eyes bulging out of the striated, red-raw muscle of his shredded face.

Slowly, she closed her eyes again.

If you're out there, if there's anything out there… help us. Please. He's going to kill us all.

And after a few minutes, when – not, of course, for the first time, but not without a sickening twist of disappointment – she had heard only silence by way of a response:

Please… I'll do anything. Just give me a sign. A sign that we're not completely fucked. A sign that there's some way out of—

She was startled out of it by a sudden burst of knocks at the door. Her eyes opened and her head snapped up, turning to the bulkhead. The wheel started spinning before she could stand out of her chair; behind her, Cale turned in his bunk, face bleary with the remnants of his interrupted sleep.

The mechanism shunted loudly and the door swung open. Diana was frozen in place, half-standing, trying not to convince herself that this was it, this was their sign, their escape…

Captain Shaw poked her head into the room and clocked them both. "You'd better come out here," she said grimly.

Diana glanced at Cale, who shrugged. She nodded, and followed Shaw silently out into the common area. Behind her, Cale swung his legs off the bed and stood up, his battered shoulder clicking loudly as he stretched. He let out a sharp breath and gritted his teeth, then followed them both.

The common area was empty. Colder than before, much colder. Diana's eyes moved to the door and she saw that it was open. The wind swirled in. "What's happened?" she whispered. "What's going on?"

Shaw said nothing, just beckoned her toward the door. Cautiously, Diana crossed the room and stepped out into the snow.

The cave walls loomed over her as she exited, sheer slopes of blue glittering with piercing banks of light. The others were all gathered out here, staring glumly at the thing on the wall opposite them. Diana didn't have to ask what they had seen; immediately she found it.

Her heart dropped into her stomach.

"Holy shit," Cale whispered behind her.

"This is why we haven't gotten out of here," Shaw said quietly. "Why we can't."

"He's watching us," Henry said, glancing in Diana's direction through the frosted lens of his broken spectacles. "That's what this is. It's a message. A warning. He knows you're thinking of escaping. Of trying to take us with you."

"He says *you can't*," Jae agreed, her voice no more than a whisper.

One of the rotor blades had been ripped from the helicopter, a flat, sharp-edged spear of slate-grey metal rent and scratched at one end, glossy with blood at the other. The bloody edge had been smashed into the icy wall of the cave, ten feet from the ground, and thick runnels of red oozed from it and pooled into the snow beneath. A network of ropey crimson strings furrowed the wall, freezing into solid veins. A gory lightning-strike fanned across the ice.

The co-pilot's body had been hung from the blade and swung gently in the wind. He had been stripped naked and most of his flesh was gone, leaving a skeleton of meat-stripped bone and the scarce knobs of muscle that remained. Through the visceral bars of his ribcage Diana could see that his heart and lungs had been removed, leaving a stringy black-edged hole within. His eyes sat loosely in their sockets, big white snooker balls of bloodshot white laser-focused on her face. His jaw was slack, clumps of brown flesh clinging to the joints, gristle and cartilage dancing in wet ribbons between the larger bones. His fingers were long and denuded of colour, his legs gnawed almost completely clean.

Goliath had hung him by a purple, frost-bitten rope of intestine, rent from the man's body and looped twice around his neck. His skull was cracked open and the little brain matter that hadn't been sucked out of him drizzled down into his eye-socket.

He *dripped*, the blood steaming as it hit the floor, then freezing almost instantly.

"Shit," Diana whispered.

Diana clapped a hand over her mouth, almost biting into her gloved palm in an effort to stifle the scream that had been building in her throat. Her eyes were fused to the bloodshot orbs in the dead man's face; she couldn't look away; even the visceral gristle-covered framework of his skeleton was just a smear of brown-grey horror through the water beading in her eyes. Tears streamed down her face, scything across her skin like rivers of ice.

A hand pressed flatly against her shoulder-blade and she yelled, wheeling around immediately. She had half-expected to see the pilot standing behind her, his flesh equally stripped, the chunks of muscle and translucent, shining organ suckered to his bones just as violently colourful in all the blue and white. Instead she saw Captain Shaw backing away, her comforting gesture withdrawn. "Sorry," Diana breathed. Looking around the huddled circle she saw the others gaping at her, startled by the sudden sound. Her chest heaved uncontrollably, hammers pounding the walls of her skull. Couldn't breathe. "Sorry. I'm sorry. I think – I think I'm having—"

She stumbled, turning to look back at the co-pilot.

He swung on the pendulum of his own intestines, the helicopter blade glinting above his head. Some of the blood flowing from the haemorrhage in his brain had fallen into his mouth and it dribbled slowly, half-frozen, over his teeth and dropped in thin strings off his bony lower jaw. He grinned madly, jaws wide like a snake's. Laughing at them.

"I think…"

Chest tight. Legs shaking, whole body trembling. She staggered back, hitting the mangled wall of the research station. Sucked at the air as every nerve in her body crackled. Looking out into the cave, she focused her attention on a horseshoe-shaped archway in the wall, through which the blue became darker and thicker: a tunnel entrance, and beyond, the entrance to the labyrinth that Dean Kirton had said, in so many words, was unnavigable.

"Everyone get inside," somebody said, the unfamiliar voice travelling to her ears through a thick wall of syrup. She had splayed her hands against the wall, her body working without conference of her mind. Her chest was about to explode. She felt shapes blurring past her but only saw the holes of their eyes: bloodshot, greasy balls pinwheeling in their sockets as they glared at her, floating disembodied above grinning, slack jaws as they flitted past. The cave dripped (water from the icicles funnelling out of the ceiling? Or blood from the body hanging from the rotor blade?) all around her.

Hands on her arms. When she turned her head, it swung as if her brain had been replaced by a heavy lead ball. She blinked rapidly, trying to get that awful image out of her mind – the face with the goggling eyes; now it twisted into a different face, the gurning maw of the titanic man in the red oilskin; now it changed again, flashing red and black and becoming the face of her father, his dog-collar loose around his neck, his stubbled jaw oily and spiny with black bristles – but it was no good, wouldn't go, can't breathe, *can't breathe—*

"Hey," said the voice again. Quieter now. Everyone else had gone. Just her and the figure gripping her arms. "Hey, look at me. It's okay. Listen. Take a breath in—"

She did, pulling in a series of hitched breaths until her throat hurts.

"That's it, now hold it – don't let it out, hold it..."

Diana shook her head. She was going to burst. Nonetheless she held it, the voice the only thing slipping through the miasma of blood and snow that pelted her head. The only thing that made sense. One; two; three; four—

"Now let it go. Slowly. Very slowly."

Mist blossomed in front of her face as her chest emptied, particle by particle, into the air.

"Again. That's it. *In...*"

She drew a breath, softly this time. The fog cleared. The face was small, slight, the eyes dark and framed by thick, black hair.

"Hold," Jae whispered. Diana clamped the air in her lungs, counting until she'd reached four. The Korean woman nodded. "Now let it out."

Diana felt the weight in her stomach dissolve.

"Again…"

She nodded. The next breath came easier: in, hold, out.

In, hold, out.

Thwum.

In. Hold.

Thwum.

Out…

Thwum.

"Better?" Jae said, her grip on Diana's arms loosening. The front door of the research base had closed behind them; it was just the two of them out here now. At some point in all the fog, Jae had turned her around so that she was no longer looking at the dead man hanging from the helicopter blade. She started to turn her head to look for it, but Jae raised a hand to her face and stopped her. "Don't," she said softly. "Look at me."

"The others—"

"—will understand," Jae said, smiling a little. Her lower lip was cracked and only now did Diana notice the bruise yellowing on her chin, the thick purple splotches on her neck in the shape of an enormous handprint. "Trust me. I've been here more than a few days. Half of them have had full-on screaming fits. I think the other half have been biting their tongues. It's okay. You're okay."

She probably had very similar marks across her own throat, Diana realised. She hadn't seen herself in a mirror since the helicopter; how much of her face was covered in dried blood?

"You have attacks like this a lot?" Jae said.

Diana shook her head.

"First one?"

A nod. All she could manage. She felt wiped out suddenly, more exhausted than before.

"It's okay. Listen, I know how difficult it is. That's it, keep breathing… it's all okay. We're in a tricky situation, aren't we? But we'll find a way out of here."

"You know about…" Diana searched for the words. She felt that she'd already found them, but saying *panic attack* out loud seemed too much to bear. "About this?"

Jae smiled. "I do. I've had 'these' since I was in college. My boyfriend at the time… it doesn't matter. He was just awful. That's all. Made me feel like I was worthless. And I think triggered something in my brain that had been waiting to come alive for a lot longer than I knew back then. Even now, I remember the things he used to do… it's difficult. I get flashes, like he's right here with me. I know what it's like to… sink into yourself."

"How do you cope?"

"I breathe, and I remember that where I am right now is better than where I was."

Diana cocked an eyebrow.

"Okay," Jae grinned. "Maybe not *right* now."

"But Henry…?"

"Yes. Better."

"You look after each other."

"We do. And that goes for everyone in there, too," Jae said, nodding toward the door. "We're going to get out of this. All of us. Okay?"

"Okay."

"You need a minute?"

"Yeah."

Jae nodded. "Don't stay out here too long. You're starting to go blue."

With a small smile and a last, gentle clap on Diana's arm, the young woman turned and spun the wheel to let herself into the base. Diana breathed slowly, waiting for the sucking sound of the door closing into its seal. When it came, she turned her head again and looked toward the tunnel entrance.

For the first time since the attack at the helicopter, she felt like she was standing on solid ground. Fists bunched at her sides, she glared in the direction of that ragged blue hole and gritted her teeth. They *were* going to get out of here.

Slowly she turned and began walking across the cavern. The icebreaker loomed gargantuan above her, a shadow of steel scything into every angle of view.

The wind was softer now, the glassy light pealing through the ice walls infinitesimally dimmer. Night was coming.

The yawing tunnel entrance opened wide as she approached. Wind howled out of the hole.

Footsteps behind her. Heart leaping into her mouth, she whirled around.

The research station was a mess of shadows and light, the immense snowdrifts leaning against it glittering as they hardened.

As she watched, a dull shadow walked slowly from the back of the ruined building to the front, carrying something long and thin on its shoulder and a black sack in its hand. Diana opened her mouth, started forward – closed it again, froze in place.

The shadow looked up at her.

Diana smiled weakly. "You must be Abel," she called quietly.

The shadow raised a hand and waved. Abel was old, bundled into a dark green coat with a thick white thatch of beard covering the lower half of his face. His hood was up; she couldn't see his eyes. But he was broad, with big hands, and the fishing rod tipped onto his shoulder was bright blood red. The sack gripped in a tight fist was squirming a little.

The old man lowered his hand, then grabbed the rod and set it against the wall of the wrecked research base. After brushing down his stomach – a small flurry of snow drifted onto his boots – he turned and walked slowly toward her.

"You're thinking about it, ain't you?" he said, nodding to the tunnel entrance.

Diana followed his gaze. His voice was gruff and quiet. She felt that he wasn't the type for conversation. "Am I stupid?" she said. "For thinking maybe we can do it?"

"Do it? You mean escape this place?"

She nodded.

"Yeah, you're stupid," Abel grunted. Diana's eyes flitted down to the black sack and she saw silvery shapes batting their tails uselessly against each other, their movements jerky and unnatural. Slowing, even as they talked. "But being smart isn't what got us to the moon."

"How'd you mean?"

The old man shrugged. Crystalline flakes of arctic punctuated his beard; his eyes were the colour of the ocean. "Being smart built the rocket. Being stupid started the space race. Tell me something: you think we'd have set foot on that thing if we hadn't had a little bit of both?"

Diana smiled weakly. "So you think there's hope."

Abel looked at her for a long time. Then, finally, he raised the sack. The movements inside were softer now, more subdued. "You think I'd be keeping that lot alive if I didn't?" he said. "Smart is catching the fish. Stupid is eating them. Same as that tunnel. Smart is knowing there has to be a way out through there. After all, there's a way *in*, isn't there? Smart is finding that way out. Smart is knowing his routines, his habits. Stupid is waiting for the right time and walking the route."

"'Little bit of both'," Diana said quietly.

"You know, some people get *stupid* confused with *brave*," Abel said.

After a moment's silence, Diana shook her head. "And?"

"They're right," he shrugged, and he turned and headed back for the wreckage.

FIVE

INTO THE DARK

Diana and Cale had gone to their cabin, leaving Henry and Dean Kirton with the rear hallway and Shaw, Jae and Megan in the common area. The three-bar had been moved so that its heat was as equally dispersed as possible. Diana had considered asking why they didn't all sleep in the same room to conserve more warmth, but supposed after a couple weeks the remaining captors had been forced to choose between warmth and sanity; they were already sharing close enough quarters, and the worst thing they could do in a situation like this was end up fighting among themselves. Besides, for every person who'd been ripped out of the research station there was another blanket; now that there were so few of them left, there were plenty of togs to go around.

Still, Diana slept with her boots on. Not because of the cold, but in case they had to run.

So, she noticed, did Cale.

Megan Hodges couldn't sleep.

Over the last couple of weeks they had settled into a routine, relying on their body clocks and a scarily-vague sense of time to determine when they ate, when they slept. There was little else to do, though, and without the waning of day into night, without the physical signals that they had all grown accustomed to, there was no way of really knowing how much sleep they were getting, how long they were awake; it was very likely that they were sleeping more than they should, because they were too emaciated to remain conscious for a full day and too terrified to *want* to. The ice navigator, Kirton, liked to make sure that they all moved around during the 'day' to keep warm, but without the space or protein this was more depleting than rewarding, and certainly didn't help them to feel less tired. They were all waiting for the inevitable, and often in utter silence. Megan felt that she had been asleep since Goliath had plucked the research base from the ground and tossed them screaming into his nest. In a constant haze of fear and confusion, she was no longer certain what was real and what might not be.

Megan needed a drink – needed a smoke, too, if for no other reason than to feel some warmth at her fingertips – but all the cigarettes were gone, and the booze had run out long before. Part of the reason she had signed on to the research mission was to get away from it all, to finally hitch herself onto the wagon by means of a sudden, sharp deprivation. It hadn't been as sudden as she'd have liked: a couple of the other scientists – dead now, God rest them – had brought alcohol, and she hadn't resisted. What had been left when they were dragged into the cavern had been squirrelled away into her belongings, and while the gin hadn't helped her to sleep, it had propelled her a little deeper into the fog for a while, and that had been a sweet and burning relief. All thoughts of sobriety abandoned, she had drunk everything.

The last drop had gone into her stomach what felt like four days ago. Certainly those days had been shorter than they were meant to be, but each one had felt like a month. She had gone cold turkey – frozen turkey – without preparing for it and with no kind of support around her. The worst thing was that she had drunk *hard*, that last day/night/whenever, and thrown up into the snow outside, and now every time she ate – though those occasions were growing sparser all the time – she brought the taste of Bombay Sapphire back into her throat and gagged on it.

She watched the others sleeping, hugging her knees against her chest. The generator was running low, and the heater's steady pulses had begun to flicker. The drumming of the generator was becoming sicker all the time, and though the smell of the vestiges of petrol didn't reach them in here, she knew that it wasn't long before it disappeared entirely. The petrol would run out before it froze, but either way…

Megan rapped her fingers against her knee, trying desperately to keep the rhythm steady so that her mind didn't run away with itself. She could feel her clothes, her blankets, her hair, like millions of needles pricking her skin. Felt the flesh itself shrivelling and tightening. She remembered the worst of it: throwing three-dozen paracetamol into her mouth and swallowing before she could stop herself; panicking and telephoning for an ambulance; lying in a hospital bed and being pumped full of acetyl-something-or-other with a fucked kidney and a fucked head… all of this when her drinking was at its worst, all of this *because* of the drinking.

And yet she wanted nothing more.

Across from her Shaw turned over in her sleep, the older woman muttering something about refusing the fine for the late return of a library book. Megan turned her eyes away from the two sleeping women and looked toward the door. Her heel tapped anxiously on the floor, the quiet thudding not enough to wake either of the others. She lowered her hand from her face; she hadn't realised, but she had been biting her nails. A greasy tangle of blonde hair obscured her left eye, but she did nothing to move it.

It wasn't the first time she had thought about it.

It would be so easy to open the door and slip out. To disappear into a corner of the cave and sit, and wait, and finally fall asleep. To be buried by the snow and have her body shut down by the cold and sink, peacefully, blissfully, into the dark. She couldn't have been the only one hoping to freeze to death rather than let the giant claim her. But she might be the only one willing to increase the likelihood of that happening. After all, wasn't it better that way?

Wasn't it better to end it now?

Slowly she stood, drawing in a deep breath and locking her eyes on the door.

At least this way, it was her choice. Hadn't she told herself she'd start making better decisions? And given all the options, wasn't this the best one right now?

Careful not to disturb the others, Megan took a slow step across the room.

Behind her the door to Cale and Diana's bunk opened and a thin wedge of light fell out of the gap. Megan froze, heart pounding in her chest as a shadow scythed across the wedge and into her field of view.

Megan turned, her mind suddenly clear and sharp. What the hell had she been about to do? Blinking, she squinted toward the open door.

"You okay there?" Diana frowned quietly.

Megan smiled. Nodded. "Just stretching," she said. Swallowing nervously, she pushed all thoughts of the cold and the cave back down into her chest. "What are you up to?"

Diana paused. Then, as if having assessed Megan's lie and found it satisfactory, she said, "I want to get everyone in here. We're getting out of this place."

There, down in Megan's stomach. The spark of

something she'd forgotten. It was something about Diana's voice. Something that lit a little something within her and told her that it didn't have to end like this. Not right now.

Hope.

"So we know he comes to the cave when he's hungry," Diana said. The lights were on – the generator was really struggling now – and everybody had returned blearily to the common area. Around her there was a brief murmur of agreement. "When was the last time he was here?"

"Before he dragged you two in here?" Kirton said. "Must have been a couple days ago."

"Tim," Megan nodded. "He came for Tim."

"Okay," Diana said. "Okay. And the last time before that?"

"A week or so, I guess," Jae said cautiously, after a moment's silence. The others ruminated on this for a minute before coming to an agreement. Before Tim, it had been Mary; three or four days before that, Iris. And anywhere between three days and a week before that, it had been Elizabeth.

"So if we assume," Diana said, "that nobody else comes along who he decides to stuff in here with us—
"

"Likely," Henry nodded optimistically. "You're the first new people we've seen in a long time."

"—then the next time he comes will either be when darkness falls, or when he's hungry again. And if it's been two days since his last feed, and he comes every three to seven days, then that gives us up to five days till he comes again."

"'Up to five'," Cale snorted bitterly. "I think you mean 'between one and five'."

Diana swallowed. "Sure," she said reluctantly. "He could be here tomorrow. He could come back in five minutes. But we have to hope for the best."

She looked around. None of the others looked particularly hopeful; she was surrounded by a sea of glumly red-ringed eyes and stubbled jaws, bruised throats and unkempt hair. They looked thin, too. The only one who looked vaguely up for it was Abel, and he hadn't said a word since she'd called them in here.

"Look, I think we can do this," Diana said, "if we stick together. Those tunnels lead *out*, they have to – that's how he's getting in here, and that's how we get out."

"They're not just tunnels," Dean said, "they're a *maze* of tunnels. How do you suggest we find our way through?"

"We move quietly, sensibly – we don't panic, and we don't run – and we leave a trail. Something we'll recognise, but he might not."

"It's got to be white," Megan said slowly, "or he'll follow the trail and find us."

"Right," Henry said, his eyes sparkling with a little

more colour than before behind his shattered glasses. "And it's got to be solid. We can't just leave bits of paper, or they'll blow away."

Abel raised a hand. "You're all forgetting something," he said quietly. "It's snow. You're *going* to leave a trail."

"Footprints," Diana breathed. She cursed. "Okay. So, if he catches onto that, he's after us. Which means we're going to have to be quick, and we're going to have to hope that he's not hungry."

"So you don't have a plan at all," came a flat voice from across the room. Diana turned her head to see Captain Shaw watching her with dull eyes, her arms folded stiffly. "Do you?"

"The plan is that we take a chance, and we stick together," Diana said.

"And once we're out there?" Shaw smiled thinly. "If he's not in the cave, he's in the tunnels. And if he's not in the tunnels, then he's out there on the ice. And there's nothing out there for miles. You don't think he's got his eyes on this place?"

Megan nodded, her stomach turning. "Even if we get out, where do we go? Compasses don't work out here, not this close to the pole. We could just head for base camp, if we knew the way, but—"

"I know the way," Dean said. He nodded confidently, ignoring Shaw's dismissive glance. "There's enough landmarks out there, I can get us to base camp."

"We'll have to be fast," Henry said.

Diana nodded. "Once we're on the ice, we can be."

Dean smiled. "I like this plan."

"It's not a plan!" Shaw said exasperatedly. "If we're going to do this, we have to be clever. Maybe we could map the tunnels, with enough care and enough time—"

"We don't have time," Diana said. "If we take our time, he'll come again for someone else. Or it'll get dark. How long do we even have, now, until nightfall?"

"A few hours," Jae said. "Then six months of darkness."

"At which point," Shaw said, "he'll go to sleep. *Then* we escape."

"Based on what knowledge?" Diana snapped. "Do we know he's going to hibernate? He's a man, for Christ's sake! Sure, a big fucking man, and one who I'm pretty sure could kill you as soon as look at you, but he's not an animal – we can't assume he sleeps at all!"

Shaw fell silent.

Diana looked around. "Look, I know everyone in here is hungry beyond belief. And tired beyond even that. I know you're all scared, Christ knows I am too. More scared than I have been in my life. We don't know where he is, or when he's coming. We don't know anything about him, except that if we run into him, we're dead. So all we can do – all we can *hope* to do – is get out there without running into him. And I think we can do that. If we go now, if we go together, then we can get out of here before he comes back. And if not... if not," she said, swallowing, "then we die. Simple as that. But if we wait here for him to come back, *we die*. Do you want to wait in here for him to come back and pick us off, one by one until we're all gone? Or do you want to come out there with me?

"I know it's a hundred times more terrifying out there than it is in here. But that thing"—she pointed to the heater—"is running out, and if you don't freeze or starve to death, you're going to be ripped apart. I know it's much the same outside, but at least there's a *chance*. Isn't there? Who's with me?"

An uneasy silence filtered across the room. For a moment there was no answer. And then, behind her, Cale cleared his throat.

"I've been in this situation before," he said quietly, his eyes locked on hers and burning. Helmand Province. Few years ago. Me and two dozen men were imprisoned and kept in a cave somewhere near Musa Qala. I couldn't tell you where. Hemmed into this iron-barred cell with nothing to eat but the scraps they threw us, nothing to smell but the death on the floor."

He looked around, his jaw setting firmly.

"Every day, the *Jag turan* would come into the cave and pick somebody. Every day at the same time. We could tell, because the cave mouth faced east. Through the bars of this grimy, stinking cave, we watched the sun rise – nobody slept – and knew that he was coming.

For a week straight, he took somebody out of the cage, marched them toward the cave mouth – never saying a word – and made them watch the sun come over the mountains before he put a bullet in the back of their head.

"On the seventh day, he left the cage unlocked. I'll never know if he made a mistake, or if it was all part of some sick plan. We never saw any other soldiers. I think he was some rogue element, doing all this on his own. He was insane, that's my theory. Driven mad by war and blood and happy to take it out on the first bunch of boys that passed by. Anyway, the cage was unlocked, and we had to make a decision. Make a break for it, or stick it out and see. Half of us left. The other half – me and eight or nine others – we stayed behind. Either too exhausted or too depressed to move, to think there was any hope. We watched our brothers sneak out of the cave and disappear into the night, and we wished like Hell we'd just gone with them. You know, maybe there *was* a chance."

He paused for a long time. The room was deathly silent.

"A few more days passed, and a few more men died. Then one fella – Peter, his name was – was walked out of the cage and to the mouth of the cave. Gun jabbed into the back of his skull. And I don't know how he did it, but the son of a bitch managed to twist that gun out of the *Jag turan*'s hand and shoot the bastard in the neck. By this point, we just wanted out. We finally had a chance, and we took it. Four of us left that cage and took everything we could from the fucker's body, then we belted it out of there.

"You know what we found?" he said, turning his eyes back to Diana. "Right outside the cave entrance, hung up with everyone who'd been shot dead in the mouth of that cave, were all the boys who'd escaped a few days before. Every single one of them, lined up on pikes. Spikes thrusting up through the bottoms of their mouths, gawping up at the rising sun. He hadn't shot these ones. We'd have heard it. And I don't know how he killed them, because we didn't stick around to look. But they were filthy, and bloody, and every single one of them had had their hands cut off and thrown into a pile. There were lizards chewing the flesh."

Diana swallowed. "Stop it."

"The only way we get out of here," Cale spat, "is if that big fucker is *dead*. And until then—"

"Stop it," Diana snapped. "Stop it!"

Turning to the others, she shook her head and tried to free herself of the awful image.

"This is different," she said. To the soldier sitting quietly behind her, she said, "I'm sorry. I'm so sorry you went through that. But this is different. We have to be the ones to escape. There's no wrestling the gun out of this thing's hands, there's no hope of killing him—"

"I agree," Shaw said suddenly, nodding. "We have to go, or die. There's no third option."

"Thank you," Diana said. "Who else? Who's with me?"

There was no time to gauge a response. Immediately after she'd spoken the ground shuddered violently, as if a sudden detonation had ripped through the cave outside. Seconds later, there was another.

"He's coming," Dean said, stumbling to his feet.

"Shit," Diana hissed. Outside another boom rippled hard into the cavern, shaking the research base. "I thought he moved quietly?"

"Not when he's hungry," Jae whispered, right before the earth shuddered again.

The research station trembled around them.

"Everyone into the back!" Diana yelled, stumbling toward the door. "Cale, get over here!"

Oliver Cale was already on his feet and stalking toward her, though the dark flash in his eyes told her that he was helping out of a sense of duty he didn't entirely agree with. "We can't hold him," he said, pushing past Captain Shaw and slamming his body into the front door beside her.

Diana gripped the frame with one hand and slammed her forearm into the door, locking her legs in place and pushing as hard as possible. There was no furniture in the base to barricade the door with, and she had an idea that he was right: the two of them wouldn't be enough to hold it closed, not if Goliath wanted in.

But they had to try.

Another titanic footstep outside – they were growing in frequency now, coming closer – and she braced herself, glancing back into the room. The scientists had started funnelling into the rear hallway and Abel was beckoning the others through, holding the door open with terror in his eyes. "Go on!" Diana yelled. "Quickly!"

A body slammed into the door and Diana snapped her head around to look. Dean Kirton pressed himself between her and Cale, the tall Black man positioning himself efficiently across the bulkhead. "Three bodies are better than two," he said quietly before she could protest.

"Good man," Diana nodded as the building shook again. In the corner of her eye she spied Captain Shaw grabbing a shelving rack attached to the wall and yanking at it, trying to wrench it free. It was welded fast. The door to the rear hallway had closed and she heard fussing and wailing behind it, the raw sounds of horror.

Something smashed into the outside of the door. Diana grunted as the wind was blown out of her, the door shuddering in its frame. It held and she closed her eyes, forcing herself hard against the metal as Dean and Cale did the same beside her.

"Brace yourselves!" she yelled. That hadn't been the creature's full force, it couldn't have been. It had the strength to drag a nuclear icebreaker across the tundra, it should have been able to blast this door off its hinges with no trouble – a barricade of bodies behind it, or not. It simply hadn't been expecting any resistance; this next hit would be *hard*.

With a scream Shaw finally managed to rip the shelving rail off the wall and staggered across the common area, gripping the thing in both hands. "Out of the way!" she yelled, marching forward to trap the rail in the door's mechanism.

Too late.

The giant crashed into the door and it flew open, slamming Diana into the middle of the room where she sprawled, then tumbled over her shoulder. Cale was punched into the wall and yelled as his spine smacked the concrete hard; Dean Kirton hit the wall beside him and slid down. Shaw had stumbled back and the pole fell from her hands, clattering loudly against the floor.

Diana looked up.

The enormous man stood in the doorway, entirely filling the frame. His red oilskin was unzipped and billowed about the barrel of his chest in the wind, and she saw that the clothes beneath were thick and tattered, as though he'd been in a scrape with something large and clawed and violent. The cables of his neck throbbed as he lowered his head to stoop through the doorframe, smiling hungrily.

There was something different about him.

"Oh, God," Diana whispered.

The nine-foot-tall man seemed to have grown even

broader in shape, his shoulders bulging against the seams of his coat, the hood lowered to reveal patches of stony skin snaking around his neck and painting his forehead. It was like the outer layer of flesh was splitting open and behind it, hard plates of grey bone were beginning to push through. His left eye was forced into a narrow slit between thick, bony lids, and the right popped angrily from its socket, flaring and jaundiced. When he opened his mouth to growl she saw that his gums had receded, shredding themselves into a pulp of purple and blue as a ring of stony chips thrust out through them – Christ, was that a *second row of teeth*?

Before she could move for the door Dean had grabbed the shelving rail and stumbled to his feet, drawing the creature's attention. It struck Diana in that moment how closely Goliath looked like somebody she knew. Aside from the greedy hatred in his eyes and the awful patches of raw stone spreading across his face, his features were average – if blown up to abnormal proportions – and she couldn't help but feel that she had seen him before. On the street, an aisle across from her in a department store, fucking *anywhere*—

If not for his size and strength and the repulsive blotches of grey knuckling up through his flesh, he would have looked perfectly, unreasonably normal.

"Get out!" Dean yelled, swinging the rail with both hands and propelling it into Goliath's face. There was a dull *crack* as the rail shot into the giant man's nose and Diana yelled, expecting him to stumble back, expecting his face to explode in ribbons of blood and bone – but nothing. It took half a second for her to realise that the sound had been the pole bending backwards.

It took another half-second for the world to explode into chaos around them.

The creature bellowed angrily, a roar of inhuman fury erupting from deep within its body and filling the room with heat. Its eyes flashed in Dean's direction and it lurched forward, grabbing the doorframe with both enormous hands. Its fingers knotted into the concrete and deep, black cracks splintered out from the edges of the frame as it clenched its knuckles, thick veins pulsing across the backs of its hands, spirals of scar tissue appearing almost soft and ballooning into each other across the wrists and fingers. The research station rocked back into the ice as the creature swung a fist in Dean's direction, chunks of rubble flung into the room when it opened its fingers and grabbed at him.

"No!" Diana yelled. Dean ducked the first swipe but Goliath was fast and thrust its arm deeper into the room, locking its thick fingers around the man's neck. The skin of the creature's forearm was splitting open, thin runnels of blood crafting intricate patterns over the skin. Beneath, more of that stony underlayer, ripping its way through. Or was it more like leather? It was the tough, cracked grey of a rhino's armour, punctuated with tiny knobs of bone—

Dean screamed as the rail was batted out of his hands and he was ripped across the room. As the creature withdrew from the doorway Dean struck out his arm and grabbed for the frame, fingers fumbling uselessly. He was too slow; his skull knocked the frame with a loud *thunk* and his eyes rolled up into his head as he was whipped out into the cavern. A bright smear of red had appeared across the top of the door.

The blood on the doorposts will be a sign to mark the houses in which you live.

"Dean!" Shaw shouted, running for the door. Diana followed and the two of them staggered out into the snow, the world shuddering around them as the creature retreated with the ice navigator in its hands.

Goliath looked back and smiled in their direction before lifting Dean Kirton high above its head, kicking and struggling, and bringing him crashing down. There was an awful *crunch* as Dean's spine smashed into the creature's enormous knee. "No!" Diana yelled again, lurching forward. Shaw's arm shot out and she grabbed Diana's bicep, wrenching her backward. Furious, Diana looked back and saw that the captain's eyes had gone wide and bright.

"It's too late," Shaw whispered.

Diana wheeled around, ripping her arm free, moved to start forward again—

She froze. Looking right at her, its narrow eye gleaming with excitement, the creature locked Dean's head in its colossal fist and *twisted*. There was another crunch of bone and a spurt of red fanned across the snow. Dean's struggling stopped at once.

"*No...*"

Goliath dropped the limp body into the snow and Diana moaned, raising a hand to her mouth as Dean was rolled onto his stomach.

"Don't watch," Shaw said, grabbing her arm again.

Diana couldn't move. Her legs were locked in place, her body leaden. She couldn't help but watch as Goliath crumpled onto his knees, shaking the world around him. for a second the great beast of a man knelt there, chest heaving, head lowered. But this wasn't defeat, she realised – how could it be? – no; he was moving into a *feeding* position.

There was a sudden blur of movement and the monster doubled over, punching its jaws into Dean's back and ripping its head left and right. Hunks of viscera were tossed into the snow and the creature ripped back its head and shoulders, slamming Dean's head and legs into the ice with both hands and rending a gory slab of meat and bone from the man's spine. Diana balked; Dean's body twitched as his vertebrae were raised through the cavernous mess of his back in a single bony cable, sheathed with a glossy film of red. The creature started to chew, blood and ichor sloughing off its chin, and then its eyes lifted again and met hers.

"We need to go inside," Shaw whispered. "Now."

"Then go," Diana hissed, shaking her arm loose. She held eye contact with the creature, forcing herself to watch as it burrowed its head back into Dean's body and threw chunks of meat and organ back into its throat. It watched her the whole time, evidently enjoying the disgust on her face as purplish strings of Dean's body drooled down its own and formed a shining wall across its throat.

When it was done, it stood. There was meat left on Dean's body, but it was sated for now. It stood.

"Now," Shaw said again. The creature took a step forward.

"Yeah," Diana nodded. "Okay."

As it took another step, they retreated, stumbling back into the ruined research base. Diana withdrew into the middle of the room and Shaw grabbed the door, hauling it into its frame. The whole wall was mangled and she couldn't close it properly, but grabbing the broken shelving rail from the floor and slipping it through the spokes of the locking wheel, she managed to prop it shut.

Stepping forward, Diana peered out into the cavern through the ragged gap between door and frame.

Goliath stood before Dean's body, the giant man's chest and legs spattered with blood, his hands loose claws. The fingers were sheathed with red. He could see her.

A full minute passed, then the creature smiled and turned around to head back out into the tunnels.

Finally, Diana let go of the breath stored in her throat. Her eyes fell to Dean's body. What was left of him lay still in the snow, steaming quietly.

For the next few minutes, there was silence. Diana heard sobbing from the rear hallway but she was numb to it, her soul separated from her body, her mind nothing but an unending reel of blood-smeared images. With every thump of her heart the reel spun again, a fresh spray of viscera searing itself onto the inside of her heart. She vaguely heard Cale behind her, telling the others through the door that it was safe now. That he'd gone back to the tunnels. It wasn't safe though, she knew that entirely now, they wouldn't be safe for as long as they were up here, and even if they managed to scrape themselves off the arctic and back to civilisation, wouldn't it follow them? Wouldn't it…

Back to the tunnels.

She remembered flashes of an earlier conversation. She tipped her head to one side, gazing out into the cavern. Closed her eyes, letting a fleet of tiny purple starships soar across the insides of her eyelids. Something deep inside told her to think back: what had they been talking about, back then? It was important. Something about the tunnels…

You're all forgetting something. It's snow. You're going *to leave a trail.*

Her eyes snapped open again.

Footprints.

"Gotcha," she whispered, and before Shaw or anyone else could stop her, she had twisted the rail out of the door's locking mechanism and wrenched it open. A blast of cold air thrust past her as she tumbled out into the snow, marching purposefully toward Dean's body.

"Diana!" Shaw yelled behind her, but she ignored the older woman, pulling up her hood as she crossed the cave. It was enormously cold, impossibly so. They didn't have long. The generator was croaking behind her now, so much weaker now that Goliath had shifted the entire base for the second time; they had to work fast.

As she approached Dean's body she was rocked by a knot of nausea and had to force herself not to vomit. She walked quickly to the limp mess of meat and bone – Dean's ribcage had been sucked out through his back and reversed, leaving a pair of spiny wings splitting his shoulder-blades apart. She knew if she slowed down, even for a second, she would stop. But she had to do this.

The blood around him had solidified already and she tramped through it, a thin crust of red cracking with every footstep and revealing a spider's-web of snow beneath. Inside, he was still warm. Holding her breath, Diana crouched and grabbed one of Dean's ribs. Hesitated. This was wrong, this was all wrong.

It's the only way.

She twisted her wrist and cracked a curved, jagged-ended rib out of place, heaving at the awful sucking sound. Hating herself every second, she dug the rib deep into the cavern of Dean's stomach. Blood spattered her arm as she ploughed the bone farther inside. Steam blossomed in her face and the stink of fresh blood, tempered by the cold, pushed into her throat.

She withdrew the rib and cringed. It was slick with blood, cool enough that it had turned thick and viscous, still liquid enough to leave a mark. She stood.

Her gaze fell onto the floor and she saw Goliath's deep, ragged footprints leading away from the body, already filling with a tiny amount of snow. The prints continued toward the tunnel entrance; she followed.

If he had gone back out there, then this was their only chance.

She moved quickly, hardly daring to look back at the research station. She could hear the others yelling for her to stop, Shaw's voice among them. It didn't matter. She had to follow him.

And when I see the blood I will pass over you, and no plague will befall you.

They might be safe in there for now, but blood froze quickly out here. And Diana had a feeling that the bloody mark over the door wouldn't mean very much to something as ungodly as the beast that had left it.

The labyrinth was long and impossibly confusing, and the footprints were filling quickly.

At every corner and every turn, she raised the bloody rib and drew a thick stripe of red into the wall. The maze was not intricately constructed but composed of a network of organic, tube-like bends, intersecting and spiralling through the tall ice fibres of what she assumed was a glacier of some kind. The light was blue and glassy; fading all the while.

The wind billowed around her as she dipped into a small side tunnel and ducked beneath a chandelier of icicles. The footprints continued down, looping around a bend to the right. Occasionally there were drops of blood. She followed the trail, marking the wall with a viscous glob of blood and careening to the right, half-running and half-staggering in the wake of the thing's footsteps. His stride was colossal and her boots sunk into his prints like a child into their father's. the light waned and swelled as she traversed the glacier's insides, panting. She was moving quickly but prayed that the creature had retained its headstart on her; to catch him up now would be devastating.

The next tunnel sloped upward and wormed to the left and she climbed, dashing the wall with another bloody mark. The whistling sound of the wind had grown so intense it was like screaming, and the cold had made her body stiff and brittle.

"Come on," she whispered, having to search the ground now. Snow swirled around her and pattered into the giant's footprints, chilling her bones as it spat into her face. Bent low she practically fell into the next tunnel, panting and exhausted, her eyes fixed on the ground. The prints were disappearing. The snow grew thicker and thicker, the prints fading, and she despaired, suddenly aware that she was going to lose him, that this was the end of the trail…

She stopped, snow beating the air, wind billowing it down the tunnel behind her. It was so cold here, so impossibly cold. She wanted to cry but knew the tears would freeze into little tracks of agony on her face. He was gone, his prints were filling in and failing fast.

But – wait – if there was snow, then surely—

Diana looked up.

The tunnel drilled open ahead of her, a vast snowscape filling the ragged mouth in stripes of billowing, folding-and-unfolding white. She laughed, unable to help herself, staggering toward the opening; the mouth-shaped archway was smooth but riddled with hanging spikes of ice, like teeth in the glacier's enormous maw. Snow blew in past the icy gums of the tunnel mouth and sprayed the walls. With one last burst of energy, Diana reached up and punched the bloody rib into the ice, leaving it propped up there as one final marker.

The arctic was sliced open across the middle, the sky above a brilliant and bloody dome of bright, blossoming red. Crimson clouds peeled away from the fading sun, its slow journey down into the tundra punctuated by banks of egg-yolk yellow. The giant was nowhere to be seen; the pole was empty.

She could run, she thought suddenly. She was here, now; she could leave the others and make a break for it.

"No," she whispered. No, of course not. She never could.

Taking one last look at the tundra, she turned her head and took a step back into the tunnel.

And froze as a great white shape slumped out of the glassy shadows behind her and growled, its lips black and thin, its eyes black and wet and flaring brightly. The polar bear was enormous, twice her height to the shoulder and brutally injured, blood spilling from a ragged gash in its side.

Unhindered by the violently-coloured wound, the snarling beast stalked toward her and lowered its snout.

SIX

THE SNOW HAS TEETH

Abel sat with his back against the wall and watched the door, rocking gently back and forth with his knees drawn up to his chest. Above him on the countertop, the fish he'd caught earlier in the day – night? – were smashed to a pink and awful-smelling pulp. His bag had been stamped on in all the chaos. Hours wasted. He wasn't upset about the fish; like everyone else, he was sick of it. He knew that it was more nutritious raw, and was in a way relieved they *couldn't* cook it; they were all deprived of vitamins and needed all they could get. The others had taken some convincing.

Not that there was much nutrition in sculpin and snailfish anyway. He caught the odd cod, but mostly the fish were small and, once scaled, hardly worth eating at all.

But if he didn't go out and catch some more soon, they would start to starve.

And he was scared.

Abel was sixty-four years old, and had only ever been scared – *truly* scared – of two things. Of course, there were the usual fears: he wasn't great with heights, though he could usually cope if he had a firm hand on something; spiders and snakes were fine, though oddly he'd always been a little wary of frogs and toads. No, these were everyday things, and he wasn't *truly* scared of them. The first thing he had truly feared, in all of his life, was *divorce*, and between oh-eight and twenty-fourteen he had been mortified of it. He had married Dora in two thousand, and for a long time they had been happy. They'd had two children – both of them living in America now; Peter worked in California as a marine biologist, and Cassie had been travelling the Bible Belt for years writing her second book – and though Dora wouldn't ever meet her, Peter would soon be the father to their first grandchild.

For six years Abel had known that Dora was hiding something from him, and for much of that time he had been afraid that that something was *divorce*. There were evenings that she wasn't home, and while that had never been a problem it started to become one when her excuses started to collide and crumble around each other; there were evenings, too, when she was home with him but her mind and soul were elsewhere. When she started to grow thin with stress he knew that he had to push her to tell him the truth, and push he did; this was his greatest mistake. He was far from proud of the way he'd been. He'd been afraid, that was his excuse. Afraid that she was leaving him. She was, of course, but it wasn't *divorce*.

The second thing that Abel was truly frightened of was *cancer*.

Dora had finally lost her years-long battle on September 13th, 2014. He never knew the truth until the very end, but he knew now that that had been his own fault. He had lived with the guilt of that for years. It had taken her from him, but even before the cancer won he had pushed her into its arms. And now he was an old man, even older than he'd been then, and he felt the weakness in his legs, felt the agony in his stomach, and knew that he was right to be afraid.

He only hoped that he'd have the chance to find her again when the cancer caught up to him too. To apologise for his weaknesses, his mistakes. To tell her how much he'd missed her.

Maybe when he found her again, they could try a second time; maybe he could be better.

Now Abel had found a third thing to fear, and fear it he did. He had seen how it ripped Dean Kirton apart. And the others. So many others…

"We should go after her," someone was saying. Megan, standing over by the door and looking out through the scar in the wall. "She's going to die out there."

Abel closed his eyes. The generator rumbled weakly, on its last legs. He needed to get out there and fix it. Find them some more food. They were relying on him. And yet he was too afraid, too weak… useless to them, now.

"It's been an hour now," Henry said, "must have been. She's dead already."

Beside him Jae swallowed, shaking her head. Their voices were like syrup, snaking fitfully through the pulsing air. "Maybe she made it out."

They were interrupted by a sudden shuddering groan, and then silence. The three-bar heater spat weakly and died.

"More blankets," Abel whispered, mostly to himself. "Generator's frozen. Need more blankets."

"I'll fetch some," Shaw said, somewhere beside his left ear, and he vaguely sensed that she'd been watching him. He opened his eyes, looking up through a bleary haze. The others were just shapes. Arguing now. Well, let them argue. Let them be afraid. They should be.

Maybe he should be grateful to that thing for offering him another way out. Was being torn in two by that creature really so much worse than being broken apart from the inside by the growths crawling through his legs and stomach?

If he had to die, wasn't it better to go out screaming than gasping for breath?

"There's no way," Henry said, poking his broken glasses up his nose. The poor kid looked exhausted. "It's waiting for her out there, it's got her by now if it didn't snatch her up the moment she went into the tunnels—"

"Stop it," Jae said quietly.

"She made it," Megan whispered. "I'm sure she did."

"Well then, she's gone and we don't need to worry about her anymore," Henry snapped. "If she's made it out, then she's done a runner, hasn't she? Otherwise, she'd be back by now."

Megan seethed. "You know how bad those tunnels are. She's lost. We have to find her…"

Their voices were all so terribly loud in the silence left by the dead generator. And it was cold. Abel felt his body shuddering uncontrollably and wondered just how long it had been doing so. Maybe this was how he went out. Not with a scream, or a gasp, but one final shake and a soft hitch in his throat as his blood froze over…

"I'm going," Jae said, and Megan nodded her agreement. "We need to go after her, make sure she's okay."

"She's dead, I'm telling you," Henry said. "We need to—"

"*Enough*," came another voice, this one low and quiet. It took Abel a moment to discern it as the soldier's.

Abel looked up, saw the young man sitting across the room from him, eyes full of steel. Oliver Cale looked around the common area, hardly shivering in the cold, hands hanging limply in his lap. His face was hard and stern, his expression as cold as the world outside.

"She's made her choice," Cale said quietly. "Leave her to it."

Abel swallowed. Silence fell across the ruined research station, and the others said nothing. The soldier looked away from them all, and for a moment Abel thought he might have seen a shred of doubt flash across his face. Then it was gone, and the only sound was the whistling of the distant wind.

Diana gaped.

The polar bear stood on all fours, its enormous shoulder rippling in the wind, shining banks of fur bristling as it stared her down with its dark, hungry eyes. It was beautiful, an animal of such enormous size and power that for a moment she was struck not by terror but by awe, by an incredible sense of inferiority.

Seconds later, the terror smashed into her.

The polar bear took a stalking step forward, growling quietly. Its lips were black and cruel and peeled back from teeth that, she saw, were chipped and bloody. It had been in a fight recently; dark red spots had soiled the left side of its face and the scruff of its neck was a mess of matted fur. Its entire left side was smeared with generous helpings of viscera, much of which had dripped down its hind leg and spotted the floor behind it; a thick, dark gouge had been ripped out of its flesh, just behind the left foreleg, so deep that Diana could see its ribs and the spongy cartilage that glistened wetly through wisps of steam rising from its torn chest.

The thing took another step, lowering its head, and Diana started to panic. She went to take a step backward but half-remembered advice she'd heard about dealing with an unexpected bear attack; half-remembering was no good, though: was she supposed to stay still, or moved *toward* it? Make eye contact, or look at the floor? And Christ, did that shit work for polar bears as well as regular grizzlies?

It didn't matter. Before she could make a decision, the bear pounced. It exploded from the snow and ripped forward, filling the tunnel in the blink of an eye and with a roar from the very depths of its belly that filled every other sense and made her insides tremble. There was no time to step out of the way; the bear smashed into her, its front paws thudding into her chest and punching her into the ice at the mouth of the cave. Diana felt a scream escape her lungs but no sound came, the air sucked out of her before it could reach her throat; gasping for air, her eyes widened as the polar bear opened its mouth wide and roared into her face, strings of drool crisscrossing her throat hotly. Black clouds flashed at the edges of her vision as the thing reared up, ribbons of agony tainting its rumbling victory cry. She took her chance and rolled, taking advantage of the lessened pressure on her chest. On her front in the snow she looked up and saw the great bear's savage maw whip toward her, its eyes burning with fury. She scrambled to her feet, clutching at her chest as she tried to drag air back into her lungs.

Holding out a hand, she croaked in dismay and shook her head. Her eyes moved to the red-raw wound at its side; clearly it was antagonised by the pain. She knew it would have broken her neck while it had her pinned if it had been thinking straight. Christ, if it was thinking straight, she wouldn't be thinking *this* – there was hardly six feet of snow between them, it could cross that distance in a second – yet it wasn't moving closer, wasn't attacking again. As she watched it shook its head and moaned, the guttural sound even more awful than its hungry roar. It stumbled, backing its rump into the wall of the glacier before turning on her again. Its eyes flashed.

The bear lurched forward and Diana ducked beneath its swinging paw, curved black claws whistling through her hair and ripping out a thin tangle. She yowled and ducked back, staggering in the thick snow at her ankles. Her legs had frozen to lead. No longer sheltered by the walls of the tunnel or the cave she was batted by the wind and the blizzard swirling at the tunnel entrance. Through slices and blobs of white she saw the blood-red sky boil with frightening energy, the last fragments of sunlight melting clouds to liquid fire that rained into the distant mountains.

The bear lashed out again with another roar,

throwing its body clumsily in her direction. Diana sidestepped, her own awkward movement becoming a half-lurching, half-running tumble that turned her back into the mouth of the tunnel. Ducking under a row of sharpened icicles, she spun on her heels and screamed back at the polar bear.

"You're hurt! Let me fucking help!" she yelled, her voice hoarse.

The bear barrelled forward, unaffected. Briefly a thread of common sense flashed across Diana's mind

(*bears don't speak English you fucking spoon*)

then her body was slammed into the tunnel wall. The wind popped out of her and she slid to the floor, gasping as something cracked inside her chest. Was that a rib? Christ, was it more than one? Her whole left side burned and she had a sudden, insane thought, pictured herself stumbling through the tunnels with the same gouge across her breast, the same ribs peering out through the hole in her flesh, the same drizzle of blood down her thigh…

The bear punched its claws into the tunnel wall above her shoulder and Diana screamed, rolling out of the way and scrabbling madly in the snow as the great white beast raked the back of her coat with an awful paper-tearing sound. "Fuck!" she yelled, leering up onto her feet and starting down the tunnel the way she'd come. She didn't want to hurt the bear – didn't think that she could, even if she *did* want to – she just had to run—

The bear was faster. She had hardly made it half a dozen steps before she heard its giant paws slamming into the ground – felt them resonating through the tunnel, more than heard them – as it lolloped easily after her. Gaining, gaining—

She yelled as its paws slammed into her shoulders and she was thrust into the ground. Snow filled her mouth and the bear lunged, opening its jaws wide to clamp them around her throat. Diana squeezed her eyes shut, preparing for the inevitable, her blood pumping loudly in her ears.

"Fuck off, Yogi!" came a voice from somewhere in the tunnel.

Something shot past Diana's head and embedded itself in the wall behind her and the bear, missing the beast's nose by an inch. A streak of black that cut through the wind like it was heated, it spooked the bear enough to make it ease off. Diana wriggled forward as the thing stumbled back, turning onto her back to watch it retreat. The thing towered over her, shaking its head, eyes wild and rabid. It was confused, pained, blood still running in thick stripes from the wound in its side. It looked at her, then in the direction of the person who'd yelled. Roaring one last time, it turned and thundered toward the tunnel mouth.

Diana watched its rump disappear in the snow then, still trying to catch her breath, looked up.

The icepick was buried to the hilt in the tunnel wall, its handle a curved lump of black steel.

Standing shakily, Diana brushed snow and blood off her coat and turned to face the person who'd thrown the pick. Her whole body shook with adrenaline and mania.

Oliver Cale stood down the tunnel from her, panting as if he'd been running.

Diana raised a hand, her fingers weak and shaking. Slowly she stumbled toward him, her legs like stone. "You saved me," she whispered as she reached him, practically falling into the man's arms. Cale held her steady for a moment, and she let herself wrap her arms around his waist, hugging him gratefully. She might have sobbed, but her tear ducts were frozen.

"Yeah," he said, his voice low, his eyes on the tunnel behind her. Watching for the bear. "You good?"

"Thick coat," she said. "I'm fine."

"Bullshit. *Are you good*?"

Diana winced. "Think he broke my ribs. Am I gonna get a punctured lung or something?"

"You'd know if you were," Cale said. "You got lucky. Looks like something got that thing pretty bad."

"Something? We both know what got—"

"Yeah," he said, pulling away from her and gripping her arms to keep her upright. "We do. Can you walk?"

"Yeah, I can walk."

Cale snaked an arm around her back and they moved slowly away from the tunnel mouth, heading for a smear of blood on the wall a way ahead. Heading back to Goliath's nest. "You found a way out, then,"

Cale said quietly after a while.

"Yeah."

"You know what's out there."

"Yeah."

"You still want to get everyone out of this cave?"

She stopped moving, removed his arm from her back. Looked at him. "We both know what's *in here*," she said. "Nothing but death, and waiting for it."

Cale gazed back at her for a moment, his face expressionless. And then, as if coming to a conclusion, he nodded. "All right. Let's get back to the others. I guess we ought to at least *try* and do what we came here for."

SEVEN

THE IDIOT'S DREAM

The generator was dead.

They had gathered in the rear hall; the front door was busted and the cold slipped easily into the common area. Out here they could huddle close together – were forced to, in fact, by the oppressive walls of the clamp-like space – and had gathered every blanket and coat to form an encompassing swaddle of warmth.

In that shared, waning funnel of vestigial body heat, they talked.

"There's a way out," Diana told them, crouched on her ankles by the door with her coat zipped to the throat and her arms folded. Her eyes were locked on the floor, unable to rise to meet any of the others'. Her body felt stiff and brittle. She couldn't remember the last time she had removed her gloves; she wondered what she would see when she finally did. "I've marked the walls."

"How?" Henry asked.

"Blood," Shaw said quietly. "The pilot's blood."

"Polar bear helped me out a little," Diana murmured. To this, a couple of the others cocked eyebrows and shared glances. She smiled thinly. "He's gone now. But we will have to be careful. It won't be easy getting out there. Less easy once we're out. But you understand that we have to do this, right?"

Abel swallowed. Sandwiched between Jae and Shaw, he had been quiet so far. He said, "We do. We're going to die in here without heat. Quicker if he comes back."

"Agreed," Shaw muttered.

"Can't say I'm on board," Henry shook his head. "He's going to catch us either way, isn't he? Why not live in relative comfort until then? Not that this is comfortable, but it's better than—"

"Shut up," Jae said, rolling her eyes. She nudged her body into Abel's, removing Henry's arm from her leg. The old man looked blankly at the young couple then turned, bewildered, and shrugged in Diana's direction. Diana almost smiled at the look on his face. In all this cold and fear, it was easy to forget that he was an old man entirely at odds with his company. She was certain he had seen Jae and Henry argue more than once, cramped together like this; she supposed that was why he preferred to be outside fishing.

"What?" Henry said, glancing around. His eyes

landed on Cale's. "I'm right, aren't I?"

Cale was silent.

"I think we should try," Megan said. "We've got a chance, then. That's all it comes down to."

"What do you think?" Henry tried again, his gaze firmly set on Cale's face. "All for it now, are we?"

Cale blinked. Looked around and saw that everyone seemed to be waiting for him to answer. Eventually, he cleared his throat and said, simply, "I've seen the way out. We can do it."

Henry's teeth closed together and he sat back, pressing himself against the wall.

Diana nodded gratefully in Cale's direction and pulled up her hood. "Now, I reckon we might be able to improve our chances a little," she said, looking at Captain Shaw. "That icebreaker you came in on. Any weapons on board?"

Shaw thought for a moment. "A couple," she said reluctantly, as if she wasn't sure they'd still be there. "Harpoons. Not sure how much use they'll be against—"

"Better than nothing," Diana said, to which Shaw nodded. "Now, we're all exhausted. Terrified. I know that. Get a couple hours' sleep, all right? We'll head out to the cave after. Half of us can find a way onto the icebreaker, and the other half can keep watch. We'll grab whatever weapons we can, then head into the tunnels. Okay? From there, it's stick together and get the hell back to base camp."

Cautious nods all around. Cale made no move to back her up on this one, but he didn't argue. She took that as the best she was going to get out of him.

"All right, rest up. This is the last night you're ever spending in this place."

The hallway was cold, but buffeted at least from the chill wind that slipped easily now into the common area. The research station – already a wreck – was falling apart altogether and it had become increasingly obvious that if they didn't leave in the morning (or what approximated a morning, when the night was six months long and the cave walls separated them from even that), they would die in here.

Diana sat with her knees drawn up to her chest and her back pressed against the wall. She hugged her calves and rocked gently, unable to sleep, afraid not to. How useful could she be, if she was worn out like this? Not to mention the pain in her chest, which had subsided into a dull throbbing but was still a deeply unsettling reminder of her encounter in the tunnels. If, upon setting off, they came across something else in those tunnels, something worse…

Faint snores surrounded her and she let her head fall back against the wall, closing her eyes again. She was too high on mania to even attempt sleep now, so she prayed. As she whispered beneath her breath, she crossed her fingers. Why not? She'd gratefully accept any shred of hope she could get her hands on. And if luck was listening, then perhaps that would be more helpful than anything else.

"If you're with us," she said, "please let this go all right. Give us strength, and courage, and just… a few more hours before you let the cold start shutting us down. Protect us if you can, from the bears, and the giant, and everything else… from whatever's out there. Please, if you can just… get us to base camp…"

She opened her eyes, letting her fingers unfold beneath her knees. Christ, they didn't even know which direction base camp was. Dean might have known, but Dean was dead now.

They were all going to die.

She turned her eyes back to the others and noticed that Cale was watching her from across the room. His eyes were flat, silver discs in the dark. "Can't sleep?" she asked quietly.

"Who you praying to?" Cale said.

Diana shrugged. "Anyone. Everyone. Does it matter?"

"I guess not."

A long silence passed between them and she looked away, made uncomfortable by the twin, shining points of his eyes. Eventually she found that she couldn't resist – she was curious, she supposed – and looked back in his direction. His gaze was still locked on her. "What?" she said.

Cale blinked. The silver discs were extinguished,

then reignited. "You don't like me, do you?" he said. "Ever since we got here. Why is that?"

Diana paused, swallowing. Then she shook her head. "I'm sorry. It's not… well, it's not you. It's… well… okay, it *is* you, a little bit. I think you've been rude, and childish, and arrogant. I'm not forgetting you saved my life in the tunnels. But if we're talking about everything leading up to that moment, then to be quite honest, you've been a colossal arse. I guess you could put some of it down to prejudice, in a way. I've never really been comfortable around soldiers. That might be on me. It's just… guns, and all that. I'm sure this doesn't go for everyone who carries one, but everyone *I've* ever met who was holding a rifle… I guess they all kind of solidified that perception. I know that's unfair. I know it is."

"You don't like me because I'm a soldier?"

"No, I mean… I was prepared to dislike you for that reason. I was. But I was also prepared to be wrong about you. And then… I wasn't. You've been rude, and oppressive, and lackadaisical—"

"Excuse me?"

"—and you threw up in the helicopter like a kid in the backseat of a car—"

"Hey, now…"

Diana clamped her teeth together. She was suddenly aware that her voice had gradually been getting louder, and she took a moment to calm herself. "I'm sorry. Look, at the end of the day, you saved my life. Like I said, I'm grateful for that. I really am. And I know I can't base my idea of you on the little time I've known you, but… that's all I've had to go on."

Another silence, and then Cale nodded. "Fair enough," he said quietly.

"I'm sorry."

He smiled weakly. "No, I mean it. That's all fair enough."

"You asked."

"I did. And you make a good point. Listen… I'm not a good example. I've spent most of my life around soldiers. Hell, even before I joined the cadets, I grew up around soldiers. Never knew anywhere I could call home for more than a couple months, but I knew soldiers. And most of them were… the best. Just the best. So don't look at me as an example of that."

"Yeah. You're right."

Cale looked away, musing for a moment as if deciding whether to continue. Then, when he spoke again, his voice was different. Low and calm, like he was talking to her from somewhere else entirely. "I used to love flying," he whispered. "I wanted to be a pilot when I was a kid. More than anything else; I wanted to fight, like my dad, and I wanted to *fly*. Then…"

He stopped again, and after a few seconds Diana noted that his breathing had changed. If she hadn't known better, she might have said he was quietly crying. "Listen, you don't have to… I didn't mean to make fun of you for getting sick on the plane. I know how hard the army must have been. Christ, after the last story you told us, I can't imagine what else you experienced out there—"

"It wasn't the army," Cale said. "One summer while I was in training, my family flew to the Galapagos. My sisters, my mum. My dad was dead at this point. Cancer. Anyway, the three of them went for a family holiday – they'd invited me, but I thought I was too grown up for all that. I thought my time was better spent with my friends. My brothers in the army. A family holiday, for someone like me – for a snotty little kid who just wanted to fast-track all the training and get out onto the front lines… anyway, they didn't make it back. My mum. Dotty, Carrie – my sisters. They spent two weeks out there. Had a great time."

He drew a deep breath.

"Their flight home… one of the engines blew. It was an Airbus A330. Went down in the North Pacific. And I still… I still can't get the sounds of their screams out of my head. Everything I saw in Afghanistan, everything I *did*… and it's those screams that I can't escape. I wasn't even there, you know? But I can't… anyway. That's why flying is difficult."

Diana swallowed. "I'm so sorry. Did you ever… in the army – did you ever have to—"

"Fly?" he said. "Oh, dozens of times. Hundreds."

"I am so sorry."

Cale smiled thinly, finally looking at her again. "It's

okay. It is what it is. These things happen, you know?"

"Cale—"

"They just happen. See, people like you and me, we're not meant to get on with each other. I know I'm an arse – and I get the whole soldier thing, I do – but it works both ways, see?"

"I don't…"

"You think somebody's up there," Cale whispered, jabbing a gloved finger upward, "listening to you. And I can't stand that. I can't stand the idea of there being somebody up there, watching all this… watching, and letting shit like that happen to ordinary people. I'll never understand how you can ask Him for help, when He's made it perfectly clear He couldn't give less of a shit about us."

Diana nodded. "Yeah," she said quietly. "Yeah, I know."

"Don't get me wrong, you believe what you believe. I'm not here to tell you not to."

"I know. To be honest… I'm not even sure I do."

"How'd you mean?" Cale said, something genuine in his voice that hadn't been there before. Diana paused before she responded, making sure the others were still asleep. Something about this conversation felt deeply private.

"My dad… my dad was religious. Heavily. Grew up on the stuff, learned everything he knew from his dad. And I was an only child, so I guess he wanted to pass it all down to me, too. I used to like it, as a kid. He'd tell me these stories from the Bible and I'd hang on to every word like it was gold. I fucking *loved* the stuff. Then I started to grow up, and I started to question things – and when my dad got the hint that I wasn't so much in love with it all anymore, he started to give up on me. The beatings – I mean, there were *always* beatings, but – the beatings got worse. He took it out on my mum, as well as me. More than he had before. The drinking got worse. It was like he thought he'd failed. He came up with a whole curriculum, I guess he thought hammering it into me a bit harder would do the job… he taught me every passage, every hymn, taught me to love God like nothing else mattered. He taught me how to make *holy water*, for fuck's sake. As if that would ever be useful."

"Holy water?"

"Oh, yeah. I can whip up a batch of that shit anytime. Tell you anything you like about Job, or Ham, or any other dummy in that book… I guess you remember this shit, when it's beaten into you."

"I'm sorry."

"I should have run from religion, after all that, but I guess I kind of found myself clinging to it. I finally got away from my dad, and I suppose… well, I suppose I wanted to look for the good in him, and there wasn't any. There just wasn't. So I looked for the good in God, and I guess I found some.

"I know it's ridiculous. I can see the problems with it. Hell, I mean, I've *seen* them. The stupidity of it. But

I like the hope. That there's something else after all this… that there's *good* out there… 'the idiot's dream,' that's what my mum used to call it when she knew he wasn't listening."

"The idiot's dream," Cale echoed quietly. "I get it."

"Yeah."

"You think we're going to die out there?" Cale said.

"Eventually," Diana shrugged.

He smiled. It was a thin smile, a dark one, but a smile nonetheless. "Good enough for me," he said.

PART TWO

EIGHT

N.S. *YAZYCHNIK*

The door was jammed so crudely into the frame that it took Cale, Shaw and Henry to wrench it open. The vast metal plate came free with a terrific mangling sound and Cale hopped down into the cave, his boots sinking immediately into a drift of snow that had heaped up against the front of the ruined research base in the hours since the creature's last appearance. Looking up, he noted tiny holes in the cave's immensely tall ceiling through which shreds of moonlight now poked and swelled. The inside of the cavern was far darker than it had been; sunset might have lasted for hours – days, even – but now that the great white orb had finally sunk beneath the horizon the darkness had very quickly replaced it. The walls had lost their glow and become a shadowy blue. The snow was colourless.

"Clear," he said, after briefly looking about to make sure the creature hadn't re-entered its nest. It was much colder than before, and he was suddenly worried about frostbite; their gloves and coats had protected them so far, but how would they fare now that the arctic cold had combined with the pitch of night to produce such an all-consuming veil of frigidity? "Come on, quickly."

He ushered out the others one at a time, helping them down from the research station – it had tipped backward a little when the giant had attacked, creating a steep ledge where before the step down from the doorway had been gentle – and out of the snowdrift. For the most part they seemed less hesitant than he had expected. This was good; the less fuss, the better.

Diana was the last out, and she closed the door behind her in a way that almost made Cale laugh. It seemed absurd, in a way, to put on even this small display of good manners, especially when they were never coming back here.

One way or another, he thought grimly.

"All good?" Diana asked, directing the question at the group. He nodded as the others murmured vague and doubtful affirmations.

"Let's go," Cale said.

They crossed the cave wordlessly, a tiny pack of dark smudges passing like ghosts through the snow. Abel hung back with Diana, his beard stiff with the cold, his eyes dark beneath the hood of his coat. Captain Shaw accompanied Cale at the head of the group, gripping an ice pick in her left hand. She seemed to have aged vastly overnight, Diana noted – a feat made even more remarkable by the fact that they could only have slept for three or four hours – and now her grey hair appeared thinner, her eyes watery, and her skin was almost translucent. Perhaps it was the dark… but no, there was something too about her expression. Where before it had been hard and resilient, now she looked weary.

Between them, Henry, Megan and Jae moved together. The scientists had been, surprisingly, the least vocal as they'd prepared to leave; Diana wondered if a part of that was down to the fact that they had known the research station as their home for far longer than any of the others. Henry in particular seemed to carry a melancholy weight on his back as they left, and she remembered that he had been one of the least receptive to the idea of escaping. She would have to watch him, she supposed, though she was certain Jae would do her share to keep him moving in the right direction. The two of them had seemed to reach an impasse before, but now they held hands tightly, sticking close together. Megan seemed twitchy, and Diana thought she recognised a look in the younger woman's eyes as the very same that her father used to bear whenever he tried to cut out the drinking. Some aftercare would be necessary with that one, Diana thought. If they made it out of here.

Cale swallowed as he led them into the shadow of the icebreaker. In the dark, all the details of the great ship had been blotted out, and it loomed over them now

as a sharp wedge of absolute black, like the night itself
had carved a trench into the cavern.

"We're all across the plan, right?" he said, glancing
back at the others. "Shaw, Abel, you're with me. Jae,
you too. We'll head up there, see what we can grab, get
back down here as quick as possible. Henry, Megan,
you're with Diana. The three of you stay down here,
watch out for Little John, and give us a sign if you see
anything."

"Got it," Megan nodded quietly. The others
murmured.

"Right," Cale said, shooting Diana one last look.
She nodded unsurely. "Up we go, then."

The rungs of a rudimentary ladder were embedded in
the hull of the icebreaker, each one frozen – not
slippery with the patina of ice that had coated it, but
rough like sandpaper – and brittle. Reaching the ladder
itself was a challenge; Cale followed the others up a
ruptured slab of ice that thrust into the wall of the
cavern, then through a series of drifts until they had
traversed the entire unstable obstacle course and made
it to the icebreaker's vast outer wall. From there, the
climb was treacherous.

As he heaved himself up the side of the *Yazychnik*,
Cale felt the enormous ship vibrating through his
gloves. Was there some vestige of power in the beast,
or were these the tremors of the ocean beneath? He

tried not to think about the other possibility – that Goliath had returned to the tunnels and was steadily approaching – but found himself unable to think of much else. Swallowing, he pushed on. Above him, Shaw had already reached the halfway point, climbing the ladder like she'd done so a thousand times. Exceptional circumstances withdrawn, he supposed she had. A little less confident but moving lithely, Jae wasn't far behind, working her forearm into each rung for extra grip and pulling herself up in a way that was almost spider-like. Cale could hear Abel breathing heavily below him and knew the old man was struggling to keep up. He had selected his group without considering the man's age; it was his skill with a fishing line that had interested Cale at the time. After all, wasn't it reasonable to assume that a man comfortable ice-fishing in the north pole knew his way around a harpoon?

If there are even any on board, Cale thought grimly.

"Here," Shaw said somewhere above him, her body lost in the great wedge of darkness that shouldered the hull and dripped over them like oil. There was a scuffling sound and Cale picked out two vague shapes wrestling in the dark over his head; from this he surmised that Shaw was helping Jae over the railing and onto the deck.

"You good down there?" he called. Beneath him, Abel slapped the hull twice with a thick gloved hand, the thumping sound of bone on metal ringing headily around them both. Too out-of-breath to talk, Cale guessed. "Good man," he murmured.

Reaching the top of the ladder after what felt like an hour, Cale let the others pull him up, folding awkwardly over the rail and straightening himself with a grunt of thanks. While the three of them waited for Abel to follow he looked around, squinting into the dark.

The deck was tilted to starboard and the ground beneath him was far from steady, canted so violently that he had to hold onto the rail to avoid falling down into the cavern below. Tall black floodlights stood dead at the edges of the deck, which sloped up toward the knife of its bow and thrummed with the beating of the arctic ocean far beneath. The floor was slick with ice, lumpen and swelling like puddingstone. A labyrinth of cargo containers, piled two-high in places, had scattered upon impact, so that the broken walls of the titanic metal maze seemed to spill toward them. Each container must have been eight feet high, with a similar width and twice the depth, and the doors of each crate were locked with a thick metal bracket. The corrugated iron walls of the storage containers, once yellow and blue and red and green, were now grey, all of them grey…

"Oof," Abel grunted as he was hauled on board. Cale turned to face the others, his gaze passing briefly over the upper decks behind them. A squat cloud radar stood battered and bent between the little group and a tall bank of thick, frosted windows, all dark. Far above the upper decks the complex silhouettes of masts and rigging structures he had no hope of understanding punched into the cave ceiling. He had no urge to look over the edge of the deck, but knew that if he did he would be sickened by the distance between him and the ground.

"What now, boss?" Jae said, hugging herself tightly as she glanced about them. She appeared surprisingly steady on her feet.

"We go for the weapons," Cale said. Turning to Shaw, he nodded. "That's your department. Where'd you keep the harpoons?"

"Two in there, for sure," Shaw said, jerking a thumb toward the upper decks. Looking over her shoulder, Cale saw that one of the storage containers had skidded all the way back across the deck and smashed into the rigging, denting the framework of the upper decks. Where some of the glass windows had shattered, snow had funnelled in, creating drifts of white inside. "More at the back, but I'm not sure we've time for all of them."

"Two is good," Cale said. "More is better. We'll see how we go."

"Right. Follow me, then," Shaw said, turning toward the battered cloud radar. "Stick to the white patches. The black is more slippy."

"Good call," Jae said, turning with some unease and stepping gingerly after the icebreaker's captain. Ex-captain, Cale supposed. Jae looked back at him, wobbling a little on the ice. "If we get out of this, I'm going to Australia or something. You don't get snow there, right?"

"You want to go to Fiji," Abel said, gripping the rail and following carefully. "Never any snow there."

"Never any snow in the Dry Valleys, either," Shaw called over her shoulder, "if you fancy trying the Antarctic next time."

"I just want to go home," Cale whispered, too quietly for the others to here. He stood for a moment watching their silhouettes struggle across the ice and the canted deck, then turned to look back toward the storage containers spilling into a brutalist fan behind him. Something struck him suddenly, something Diana had said earlier. Hours ago, now. Before the tunnels, maybe. Something about the icebreaker.

God, what *was* it?

His eyes fell onto the nearest container. The bracket holding the door was bent and broken, twisted out of shape, and the door itself had fallen ajar. A wedge of pitch black peeled up the edge of the container, giving away nothing inside. But there was a smell, he realised, made metallic by the cold but nonetheless recognisable.

Christ, what had she *said*?

"Hey," Cale called suddenly, his voice stiff. "Hey, Captain. What were you lot shipping up here, anyway?"

He kept his eyes on the container, as if they might adjust to the dark spilling from it. Behind him, Shaw paused. Turned to look back. "I don't know," she said. "The cargo was loaded and we were given a heading. Our client was meant to meet us out here and unload everything, but nobody ever showed."

Cale took a step toward the container. "And you don't know what's in any of these?"

Watching him carefully, Shaw shook her head. "We don't ask. We just do the job."

"Your client," Cale said, taking another step. "Who are they?"

Shaw paused. "Uh, I don't remember. It's been a hell of a week. Or however long. Some Swedish company. Sounded Swedish, anyway. Uh… oh, *Astarte beg*. Something like that."

Cale approached the container cautiously, as though he expected something to jump out of it any moment. As he moved the narrow black wedge seemed to widen, yawing open like a hungry mouth. That smell… oh, God, that *smell*…

"We should go," Abel called. "The harpoons. Quickly."

"Yeah," Cale said quietly, reaching for the door. Even through his gloves, the metal was immensely cold to the touch. "I'm just… curious…"

The hinges were stiff, but with a sharp tug the door opened enough for him to see inside. It was impossibly dark inside the container and he stepped forward, close enough for the smell to invade his nostrils and clamp itself to the back of his throat.

Frozen meat.

He gritted his teeth as he surveyed the misshapen silhouettes inside the crate, every muscle in his body tensing. His hair might have stood on end if his skin weren't already coated with gooseflesh. Tiny slivers of moonlight, refracted through layers and layers of ice above them, sliced through dozens of small reflectors in the container, each an inch or so in size, all arranged in pairs…

"Bodies," he whispered. The container was piled high with bodies.

The smell followed him as he stumbled back, looking up into the labyrinth of containers. There must have been thirty or forty of the things, each one filled with flesh. His eyes turned back to the container in front of him: there were men and women inside, maybe fifty of them. Some of the bodies were smaller, but he didn't think about that. Tried not to, at least. They had been stripped, and a crust of snow filtered between them, runnels of ice pooling between splayed legs and into open, silently-screaming mouths. This container was only half-full, and now that he was looking – really looking – he saw that some of those closest to the door had been ripped apart. Some had limbs missing, some heads.

He turned his head, staring wide-eyed at Shaw and the others. "Your client got their delivery," he called, his stomach churning with nausea. Staggering away from the crate, he shook his head, trying to push the vomit back down his throat. "Ohh... oh, shit. This is nasty."

"What is it?" Jae said, starting forward. Cale raised a hand to stop her.

"Food," he said. "Dean was right about this thing. It's going into hibernation. And it needed a store of food for the long night. A store of meat."

"Oh, God," Abel whispered.

"No," Shaw said, "we would have known, we would have—"

"You didn't," Cale said, "but now you do. And we have to get out of here. We're... oh, shit. Oh, *shit*. We're in its fucking *pantry*."

Somewhere far below the icebreaker, somebody whistled.

Henry Pochetty gazed back at the research station and wished he'd stood his ground.

Beside him Megan was looking furtively around the cavern, her arms folded across her chest to conserve warmth, her body stiff and hunched and shivering. Diana had been pacing but now she stood stock-still, staring at the tunnel entrance. Both of them looking for the giant, waiting for him to appear. What the hell were they going to do if he *did* come? Henry wondered bitterly. They'd split up now – the last thing anyone ought to do, he thought, in this kind of situation – and abandoned their home base, the only thing that had kept them safe so far. All right, it hadn't kept *everybody* safe, but at least they hadn't been freezing to death.

Are you forgetting the generator's busted? he scolded himself. *The only reason we* didn't *freeze to death is useless now. You'd be just as fucked in there.*

Still, he felt vulnerable out here. Exposed. The wind grew stronger the closer they came to the tunnel entrance and here, standing between it and the icebreaker, they were so violently, cloyingly enveloped in the colossal ship's shadow so that they could hardly see a few feet in front of their eyes. Henry could feel his hands and feet numbing. The longer they stood around here…

"You see anything?" Megan whispered. Behind them the *Yazychnik* seemed to creak and shift, as if the movements of the four on board would bring it tilting down any moment and take the whole cavern system with it. He was imagining it. Must have been. The ship had withstood the beating wind for long enough; what difference would four tiny, insignificant bodies make?

"Not yet," Diana said, "but keep watching. We'll need to signal the others if he—"

"We know," Henry spat. "Keep quiet, both of you."

"Christ, what's got into you?" Megan hissed.

"I don't want to die," he said simply, turning away again. The research station was little more than a hunk of shredded metal in the distant reaches of the cave. The shadows draped across its mangled roof were like thick, monstrous claws. His eyes lifted, following the shadows up the curved wall of the cave. The blue was marbled by the faintest traces of moonlight trying to seep through the ice; instead of breaking into the cavern they created spangling networks of white and grey among the whorls and smears of dulled cobalt.

"We need to get them back down from there," Diana said anxiously, her gaze locked on the tunnel entrance. "He's going to come through any minute, I can feel it."

"It's okay," Megan said quietly, taking Diana's hand in her own. Henry continued tracking up the wall, his eyes flitting from icicle to icicle, from slope to slope, up, up, up… "It's okay, if he comes back, we'll be ready. They're going to be back any minute, and they'll have weapons, and we'll fight him. We're going to get out of here."

Henry swallowed, his head tipped back, his eyes moving across the ceiling now. The shadows seemed to move and swell in the half-light of the moon, bending and breaking as he watched.

Something slunk between the shadows and his whole body froze as he watched it pass across the smooth surface of the ceiling, moving like an insect.

"Uh, guys," Henry whispered. "Look up…"

"What?" Diana said. "What is it?"

"Oh my God…"

The creature stalked across the ceiling, using its

enormous fingers to dig handholds in the ice, climbing expertly despite its size.

Henry dug his finger and thumb into his mouth and whistled sharply, the piercing sound echoing through the cavern. The creature seemed to hear it and started to scrabble faster across the ceiling, almost snaking over the ice, two tiny points of moonlight boiling in its head.

It was heading for the *Yazychnik*.

"Go!" Cale yelled, the whistle still echoing in his ears.

The icebreaker shuddered as the colossal shape plummeted off the ceiling above them and slammed into the deck, landing on all fours like a rabid dog and slipping in the ice, crashing into the wall of one of the storage containers. It left a dent. For a moment Cale just stared, his mouth open, throat dry and useless. Goliath seemed to have grown larger since the last time they had seen him, his massive shoulders doubling in size, his neck and chest rippling with striated muscle. He had abandoned the coat – he was naked, Cale realised with horror – and his flesh was lambent and red. In places the skin had ruptured open and saw-like bony protrusions had thrust out, ripping directly out of his skeleton to form spines up and down his back. Slowly the creature looked up, eyes flaring yellow.

"Run!" Cale screamed, stumbling back from the thing. The creature bellowed, the skin around its mouth cracking open as its maw split into a ragged black cavern. Thin beads of glossy black blood ran down its neck and more bony knots pumped up through the bloody crevices. Even as Cale watched the thing was transforming, shapeless and awful, thick plates of stone popping out of its back and shoulders like armour and peeling away the skin all around them. He staggered, almost slipping in the ice, and wheeled around to follow the others. Abel was frozen, still gripping the rail, and Shaw stood speechless beside the broken radar dish. "For God's sake, *run!*"

Cale grabbed Abel by the arm as he thundered past and the two of them ploughed forward across the ice. Jae's eyes were locked on the creature and Cale could almost see the scream building in her throat.

"Go! Go! Go!" Finally she started to move, turning in slow motion and almost falling into Shaw's arms. The two of them tumbled into an awkward run down the canting deck and Cale let go of Abel's arm, shunting the old man into second gear as he turned on his heels and looked back. "Go, I'm coming!"

The creature rose onto its hind legs, towering above the nearest container. It must have stood at twelve feet tall, even hunched like that with its head and neck lowered, its shoulders ripped into knots of stone and broken flesh. Strings of blood swung from its lower jaw, eyes burning points of yellow fire.

"Oh, shit."

He turned and pitched forward, grabbing Abel again

and yanking the old man toward the upper decks. The bank of windows above them was spotted with patches of frost; directly ahead a tall iron door was embedded in the structure, its frame peppered with enormous boltheads and sprayed with rust. He practically threw Abel toward the door and steadied himself, skidding forward on the ice.

The ship rumbled as the creature took a heavy step toward them. Jae screamed from somewhere over his shoulder and Cale looked around, desperately scanning the dark. He found her as the creature took another step, the deck jouncing violently with the impact. His eyes widened as he watched Jae tumble onto her back, sliding in the ice and grabbing for a handhold – there was none, and she rolled awkwardly, shrieking with agony.

"No!" Shaw yelled, starting to change course.

"Get that door open!" Cale shouted, grabbing the older woman's arm before she could start toward Jae. "Get inside, both of you, now!"

Shaw nodded, backing away as the creature took another step. Cale's eyes flitted from Jae to the beast and he saw that it was heading for her, that it had picked her out as the easiest target. *No. No, no, no...*

"Get up!" he yelled, starting forward. The cant of the deck and the thick layer of ice made climbing it hard and his legs burned as he powered forward, trying and failing to launch into a run. It felt as if the whole icebreaker had been tipped backward another forty degrees. Twenty feet from him Jae scrambled to her feet, her eyes on him, wide and wet and pleading. He lunged, one hand outstretched to grab the girl, every fibre of his body screaming in pain and terror. "That's it, come on! *Come on!*"

He was four or five feet from her when the monster swiped Jae off the ice, curling the fingers of one enormous hand around her midsection and lifting her easily into the air. Cale stumbled, gaping upward, fury broiling in his throat. "No!" he screamed. "Put her down, you big fuck! You put her down *right fucking*—"

Jae howled as the beast squeezed, her ribs cracking audibly. She flailed, her back arching as she tried to wriggle out of Goliath's fist. The dreadful creature seemed to grin, its jaws splitting open, the ragged bony mandibles piercing its face and neck extending into vicious, stone-coloured claws. Before Cale could take another step the thing had raised its free hand into the air and it splayed all five fingers, preparing to strike.

"*Jae!*"

Goliath slammed the heel of his titanic hand into Jae's chin and there was a sick, echoing *pop* as her skull was shunted off the top of her spine. Her eyes went wide one last time, bulging in her head as it was violently adjusted from her neck. Her hair billowed about her like an ink-black halo in the moonlight and Cale yelled, anger and guilt and pain exploding from his chest all at once.

The creature dropped Jae to the deck and she flopped limply at its feet, her chest deflated where the ribs had been punched into her lungs, her head sitting loosely on her neck at an angle that made Cale want to throw up. Behind him he heard the metal bulkhead door opening and Abel screaming for him to follow them, to get away from the creature, but he couldn't stop himself from watching the awful spectacle unfold. Jae was still alive, he realised sickly, trying to speak but finding the cords in her throat suddenly unconnected, croaking like a newborn animal trying to bleat. Staring at him.

The creature stamped down a stony heel and her head exploded into a fan of pinkish pulp, spraying the broken radar dish. Cale felt a spatter of fluid slop against his shins and balked, staggering backward, eyes locked on the woman's convulsing body.

"Come on!" That was Shaw. "There's nothing you can do, leave her!"

"Run, man, get inside! You can't help her now, for God's sake!"

Cale tumbled back, almost falling onto his rump, somehow managing to manipulate the fall into a jerky half-run. Behind him the deck shuddered and a sudden certainty punched into his body; it would be him next if he didn't move, it would be his ribs breaking in the thing's gargantuan fist, his skull knocked off his body, his—

Abel grabbed him by the coat and yanked him

through the door. Shaw slammed it behind him with a colossal bang and the three of them fell against the wall, panting and heaving. Cale yelled as the creature smashed into the door behind them, the entire icebreaker shaking with the impact.

"Harpoons," Cale breathed, and Shaw nodded.

"This way."

She pitched into the corridor and Abel lunged after her. Cale yowled as the creature punched its body into the door again, the impact knocking several discs loose up and down his spine. Staggering into the corridor he followed the others, resisting the urge to turn his head toward the window and look back out onto the deck. He didn't need to see her again, her ribs all sunk in like that, her head and shoulders stamped into nothing…

Shaw led them around a corner and Cale glanced back as he turned. Down the end of the corridor, the door imploded and a ragged wedge of moonlight sprayed the opposite wall like a shotgun blast. The creature swung an arm through the opening, swiping with those giant fingers.

"Help me with this!" Shaw yelled, her voice travelling to him through a throbbing, booming wall of blood-sound. He snapped his head around to follow the voice and lurched forward, tumbling down the corridor toward her. The captain had found another door at the end of the corridor and was struggling with a frozen locking wheel, her teeth gritted, face red with cold and fear. "Come on, damn it!"

An enormous explosion of sound behind them and the icebreaker shuddered again as the creature forced its way into the corridor. It roared, the guttural bellow travelling like floodwater down the hall and filling every one of Cale's senses. He pushed past Abel and grabbed the wheel with both hands, yelling out as he and Shaw tried desperately to rock it open. The mechanism was frozen and he could hear metal bending as they forced the wheel round, inch by inch, millimetre by millimetre—

"It's coming!" Abel hissed behind them, and a shadow fell across the door. Cale could smell it, smell the blood on its hands, fresh – not frozen like the meat in the containers – fresh and warm and dripping.

"Help us!" he yelled, and Abel stumbled toward the door. The corridor shook as the creature bent forward, taking a heavy step toward them. Enjoying the chase. *Don't look at it*, Cale thought, *don't look—*

"Quick!" The wheel spun suddenly, the mechanism breaking and the tumblers falling over each other as the door collapsed inward. The three of them tumbled inside just as the creature swung an enormous paw at them and Cale yelled, jagged nails whistling past his cheek and ear, drawing blood. He slammed the door closed and started to spin the wheel, hoping that there was enough of the locking mechanism left to keep it closed for a minute.

"Christ!" he yelled as the creature slammed into the door and he was blown backward. He tumbled onto his stomach and looked up to see Shaw running to a bank of controls across the room. the far wall was all glass, thick metal supports punctuating what was otherwise a long, frosted window like bars across the window of a giant's cell. His perception of colour and shape was off and he felt like he was swimming. Watched as Shaw ducked beneath the control panel, disappearing. Abel going after her. Cale's head swung back toward the door.

It sailed toward him and he yelped, ducking his head as the beast smashed its way inside. The twin points of its eyes blazed like molten metal and it bellowed again, looking around the room. Cale scrambled to his feet and staggered across to the control bank where Shaw had disappeared. "Out," he yelled, "we need to get *out—*"

"You need to get *down*," Shaw said quietly, appearing again and swinging something long and steel-grey into view. Cale's eyes widened and he ducked beneath the thing, grabbing the control bank for support. He felt a hand on his arm and let Abel pull him to his feet, the pair of them moving clumsily toward the nearest window.

Shaw pointed the harpoon into the creature's face and fired.

There was a deafening *click* and she swore loudly. "Forgot how to load the fucking thing!" she yelled, struggling with the harpoon for a moment. Goliath took a step toward them, crossing half the room in a second. Glancing at Abel, Cale saw that the old man had a second harpoon in his hand; both of them *looked* loaded, but Christ knew he hadn't the foggiest when it came to these things. "There's no time," he yelled, turning back to Shaw. "Get back!"

The creature took another step. The room swayed, buckling around them. Shaw was fumbling with the line, the foreshaft of the harpoon gripped tight in one hand, her face lifting to the beast as it towered above her. He saw her pause.

"Abel, go!" he yelled. Beside him, Abel was already moving. Cale lurched forward, grabbing Shaw by the coat and yanking her out of reach of the creature's swinging fist, then before she could protest they were skirting around the thing, back the way they'd come, heading for the mangled doorframe.

"Just give me a second, I can get him!" Shaw yelled.

"Not right now!" Cale yelled back, shoving her through the door. They pelted up the corridor, the floor no longer smooth but thoroughly dented where the massive creature's heavy steps had bent the metal. He could hear it coming after them, turned to look back, slammed into the wall. Grunting, he forced himself around the corner and followed the others out the door.

The cold blasted him, ice suddenly under his feet. Abel was waiting by the rail. "We have to jump!" the old man yelled.

Cale grabbed Shaw's hand and dragged her forward, still struggling with the harpoon gun. "Come on!"

"We can't fucking jump down there!" Shaw yelled as they reached the rail. Cale looked down and forced down the vertigo that swelled in his skull. He shook his head, eyes locked on the snowdrift below. It looked soft enough, but Christ, it was a long way down—

Wind batted him as he turned to Abel. "You first," he said.

Abel shook his head, gripping the harpoon with both hands. "Mine's loaded," he replied, eyes steely and determined. "You two first."

"Okay. Jump," Cale said, grabbing Shaw's arm. "Now."

Shaw stared at him, face white as bone. "I can't," she whispered. "I just can't—"

"You can," Cale said, and he reached for her hand. "Come on, together then."

He heaved himself over the rails, still holding her hand. Practically dragging her over, he nodded back at Abel. "You too, old man."

Abel grinned. "Yeah, I'm coming. Don't you worry about me."

Then they tipped forward.

For a moment Cale wasn't entirely sure what had happened – had he pulled Shaw? Or had she been overcome by a sudden burst of bravery, and pulled him? – but then the moment was gone and his whole body smashed into a wall of snow that was far more solid than it had looked from above, knocking all the wind out of him and making him wheeze. Shaw punched into the snow beside him, narrowly avoiding spearing her midsection on the harpoon blade in her hand.

Cale staggered to his feet, the ground beneath them unsteady and shifting. "Abel!" he yelled, his voice lost immediately to the wind twisting through the cavern. "Get down here!"

A shape appeared at the rails and he stumbled back, preparing to try and catch the old man as he fell. Gazing up, Cale watched as the silhouette keened backward, lurching through the air, separating with the wedge of black that was the icebreaker's hull—

Then a great stony arm shot out of the grey and snatched the silhouette out of the sky. There was a sick, wet *crack* and something plummeted toward them, something thin and black—

"Get back!" Shaw yelled, grabbing Cale and dragging him back into the snow.

Abel's harpoon buried itself in the drift at his feet, sinking halfway up its shaft. It was followed, seconds later, by a slimy fan of blood.

NINE

OLD TONGUE

Diana lunged forward as the icebreaker rocked, yelling Cale's name into the cavernous blackness before them. "No!" Megan yelled, grabbing her arm and pulling her back. Diana struggled, trying to bat her away, then realised Henry had grabbed her other arm too. She shot him a sharp look and saw stern, horrified resolve in his eyes.

"You can't," he whispered.

Diana wrenched her arms free and staggered forward a step, her knees threatening to give way beneath her. She stared at the *Yazychnik* as a final scream trilled through the air, almost soft and pleasant. Like the jangle of wind chimes, bouncing off the icy walls. For the past few minutes the yelling had been incoherent and faraway. This last scream felt close and piercing.

"We have to get up there," she hissed, "we have to—"

"Look!" Megan called, jabbing a finger in the direction of the ship. The thick oily wedge of black that was its hull seemed to tip back as, beside it, a flank of grey shadow yawed open. "It's them, it has to be!"

Diana's eyes widened as a pair of silhouettes exploded from the shadows, hurtling toward them across the cavern. "Come on," she breathed as the two shapes began to clarify, peering into the dark behind them for the others, "come on, come on…"

A third silhouette appeared. Larger than the others – a lot larger. Diana's heart sank into her stomach. "Jae," Henry whispered beside her. "Where's Jae?"

The silhouettes took on form as they came closer. Cale and Captain Shaw, both of them brandishing a silver harpoon gun. Shaw seemed to be twisting the harpoon into the shaft, a thick cable looped around her wrist. Cale turned, staggering backward, eyeing the enormous thing that had followed them off the icebreaker. "Everyone to the tunnels!" he yelled.

The giant stepped forward and the cave trembled. Goliath was changing, Diana realised with awe, blood pumping loudly through her body. His face was stony, riddled with bony spines and hooks, his back and shoulders slate-grey and covered with thick, nobbled plates. He strode confidently across the ice, his body exposed to the cold, his muscular legs ripped open to reveal bloody tangles of stone beneath the broken flesh. A thick thatch of white hair covered Goliath's chest and groin, matted with blood. His mouth was red and grinning.

"Jae!" Henry screamed, pelting forward. Cale's hand slammed into his chest and the two of them fell back. "Where is she, damn it? Where the fuck is she?"

"She's gone!" Cale yelled, grabbing the man's arm. Spittle flew from his mouth as he spoke, his own face spattered with blood too. "I'm sorry, man, she's gone!"

"Abel…" Diana whispered. Shaw shook her head.

"Fucking shoot it, for Christ's sake!" Megan yelled, backing away as the beast roared, taking another long, loping stride toward them. Its face had changed but the expression was still human, yellow eyes blazing in a twisted mask of cruelty.

Shaw wheeled around, slamming the butt of the harpoon gun into her shoulder and closing one eye. She gripped the shaft firmly, the barbed point of the weapon pointed at the creature's throat. "Everyone get back!"

Goliath roared forward and raised both fists above its head, preparing to slam them down. As it did, the thick sinews stretched across its armpits snapped, more stony spikes butting through the wounded flesh. With a dreadful scream – half pain, half fury – it took another step and its eyes flickered brightly in the sunken pits of its face.

Shaw squeezed the trigger and the harpoon exploded out of its shaft, sailing forward on a thick, whistling streak of cable. She had overcompensated for the kick and its trajectory was too low, far too low;

Diana watched helplessly as the harpoon shot into the creature's thigh, punching through meat and blowing a great wing of thick, black blood out of the thing's leg.

"Fuck!" Shaw yelled, grabbing the cable with one hand and stumbling back, trying desperately to tug the harpoon free. The giant keened backward a little as its leg was yanked from beneath it, then reached down with a single fist and ripped the silver spear out of its flesh, tossing it into the snow like a toothpick. Diana caught sight of more stony nubs screaming out of its injured thigh, but her attention was on Shaw. She rushed to the older woman and grabbed at the cable, helping her to pull the harpoon back across the ice.

"Your turn, Cale!" she yelled over her shoulder. The man was already preparing to fire his own harpoon gun, raising it high and stepping forward to brace himself against the butt of the thing. The beast was bellowing again and this time Diana froze, drawn strangely to the sound – there was something different about it – no longer an animal roar but a conscious string of twisted roars that almost sounded like…

She turned, her eyes widening.

"Stop!" she yelled.

Cale's finger snapped away from the trigger and he turned to look, thick hair falling in his face. "What?!

The creature was staring right at her, its eyes burning hard, its mouth twisting into awful shapes. It was speaking, she realised, that awful booming coming from its chest forming words and sounds that were far more than any hungry roar she had imagined it capable of. Not English, though. The language it spoke was far more obscure, far more ancient…

"It's Aramaic," she whispered.

"What?" Cale yelled again. Shaw had stuffed the harpoon back into the gun and was swinging it into her shoulder. Beside her Megan had grabbed Henry's arm and the two of them stared open-mouthed at the beast with the bloody arms and the gnarled roots of bone and rock punching out of its flesh. It seemed to have doubled in size.

"Give me that!" she called, reaching for Cale's harpoon.

"You think you're a better shot than me, now?" he yelled, pushing his finger back through the trigger guard and taking aim again. "We only get one chance at this, lady!"

The creature took a shuddering step toward them, hardly fazed by the oily blood running down its leg. It was still speaking, gazing up at the ceiling now with its titanic hands spread wide, as if praying to something up there. That ancient language rolled harshly off its tongue, forming words Diana didn't know, couldn't hope to understand. But her father had tried teaching her Aramaic once; nothing had sunk in, not the words themselves, but she knew the importance of this, or hoped she did at least—

"Just give me the fucking gun!" she yelled. Turning to Shaw, she said, "You too! Now!"

Cale swore and swung the harpoon in her direction. As Shaw did the same the beast took another step, shaking the whole cavern, towering over them, a sentinel of Biblical proportions.

Biblical.

She gripped Cale's harpoon by the shaft and grabbed Shaw's, holding one in each hand. They were heavy, ridiculously so, and she realised suddenly that she hadn't used her arms for very much in the time since they'd arrived. Ignoring the sudden ache across her upper body she took a confident step forward – toward the approaching creature – and yelled, "Hey! Down here, ice-fucker!"

The creature's head swung down and it looked hungrily down at her through narrow, shining eyes. If this thing was as old as it sounded – if there was any hope left in the world…

"Look at this!" she yelled, and she raised both harpoons before her face, slamming their shafts together to form a barbed, oversized crucifix. There was a dreadful clang as the harpoons joined, and for a moment she was blinded by the spear of refracted moonlight that seemed to lance down and blast the centre of the shape. "*Am I speaking your language now, bitch?!*"

The creature roared in agony, the sound almost mournful, taking a staggering step back and raising a giant hand in front of its face. Through the gap between its fingers Diana saw those awful yellow eyes flicker like dying candles, then it turned its head violently away from the glinting crucifix and took another step back, as if hurt.

"*Ha!*" Diana yelled, stepping forward. She braced the heavy cross above her head, forcing her arms to work despite the cold ache thrumming through them, turning the crude shape into the path of the faint moonlight. "You don't like that, do you?"

"We have to go!" Cale yelled. She glanced back and saw Shaw furrowing the others toward the tunnel entrance. She nodded, turning her head to look back at the creature.

Two flaring points of yellow blazed in her direction through the thing's splayed fingers. As she watched, it curled its massive hand into a fist and growled.

Lowering both harpoons, Diana stumbled backward. "Yeah," she said. "Time to run."

TEN

POLAR ANIMALS

A vortex of blue-grey whorled past them as they lurched into the tunnels. The giant's footprints had been filled in and beaten away by the wind, but the bloody marks on the wall had remained, albeit brittle and frosty and frozen-meat pink.

Captain Regina Shaw led them quickly, her harpoon back in her hands. It was heavy and her heart was fluttering weakly, her legs and arms thick with exhaustion. Diana had taken the rear, brandishing the second harpoon, moving backward and swinging the shining spear of the thing left and right into the vast drillhole of the tunnel behind them. Somewhere back there in the dark, the creature bellowed again and the sound echoed, funnelling past them, causing hollow chunks of ice to fall from the ceiling. Shaw glanced back as they careened around a violent bend, performing a quick mental headcount: the others were little more than silhouettes in the darkness of the tunnel, but she could make out the two remaining scientists and Cale, as well as Diana and the shining third arm of the harpoon carving brilliant, glinting arcs into the dark. "Come on!" Shaw yelled, slamming her back into the wall to let Henry and Megan past. They ploughed forward, the tunnel floor sloping upward, the wind growing stronger as they propelled themselves unrelentingly forward, desperately forward. "Diana! Any sign?"

Cale grabbed Shaw's arm and the two of them ran after the scientists, Diana nodding behind them. "It's in here!"

"Can you see it?"

Diana couldn't, not yet, but she could feel it. Knew that the others could, too; every powerful footstep shook the length of the tunnel, dislodging more shivers of ice from the walls, sending Diana's heart into her mouth every time before it had the chance to fall back into her chest. "Not yet," she yelled, "but we need to hurry!"

Shaw pulled her arm free of Cale's grip, running alongside of him, her boots sinking into softer snow. They must have been closer to the tunnel mouth now, for she could feel the icy thrill of the wind outside; back in the cave it had slipped through holes and cracks in the ceiling, but here it punched right into them. Her chest hurt, more than ever. She had been doing her best over the last few days to keep the stress to a minimum – not easy, when you were surrounded by the dead and terrified and being hunted by a demonic Bigfoot-Yeti-thing – but now it was at an all-time high and she was afraid her heart might actually give out again. She had suffered two heart attacks in the last ten years: after the first, she had been fitted with a stint, but of course that had failed and caused the second, and now she was on so much anti-anxiety medication and pain relief – so much that she *hadn't been able to take* since Goliath had dragged her and the rest of the icebreaker crew into its nest—

"Agh!" Diana yelled as an enormous shadow exploded from the tunnel behind her and raked its fingers across her stomach. Shaw turned her head, eyes widening as she saw the harpoon fall from Diana's arms into the snow. Cale had dropped back and she swung her own weapon around as the creature roared again, appearing out of the dark, bearing down on Diana as she tumbled to the ground.

"Diana!" Shaw yelled, but already Cale had dug his hands into the snow beneath her and scooped her backward. The creature's fist smashed into the ground between her legs and hot, red spittle sprayed her stomach as it snarled viciously. Its fingers were stony and grey, the knuckles piled on top of each other like sharpened pebbles in a bag – or teeth, dozens and dozens of bony, serrated teeth – and blood filtered through cracks in its rocky skin like water. It was no longer human, so violently transformed that it seemed to have become some kind of golem-like beast, its wrist plated with rocky armour, its forearm knotted with chipped spikes.

"Run!" Cale snapped, grabbing the harpoon as Diana scrambled to her feet. Shaw backed up as the two of them turned and hurtled away from the giant, its body filling the tunnel now, its jaws open and hungry, eyes providing the only light. Shaw grabbed Diana's hand, gripping her weapon in the other, and together they ran.

"This is it!" Megan shouted from somewhere up the tunnel and the three of them followed her voice, running hard into the wind. The beast moved slowly behind them, grinding its feet into the ground, arms outstretched so that it could drag its mottled claws through the icy walls, gouging out ribbons of white and letting them filter into the bloody snow behind it like pencil shavings.

A pinhole of light appeared ahead and Shaw grinned, pushing Diana ahead of her. "Come on!" she called back, glancing over her shoulder to see Cale turning and running after them, the harpoon swinging in his arms. Behind him the creature had disappeared. She frowned. "Where did it go?"

"Down another tunnel!" Cale said, out of breath. "Let's go!"

Shaw drew a sharp breath and lurched forward, the three of them heading near-blindly for the tiny flickering patch of oily moonlight at the end of the tunnel. She could hear the scientists up ahead, Megan calling back to them while Henry ran to catch her up. The giant's footsteps had faded, the rhythmic vibrations jolting the tunnel growing smaller until they were gone altogether. The tunnel mouth grew clearer and she grinned, ignoring the complaints in her chest and pushing herself harder. They were nearly there, nearly out, nearly *free*—

The ceiling ahead of them exploded in a shower of white and Shaw was blown back as something leapt down into the tunnel from above, a colossal shadow with massive hands and unblinking yellow eyes. "Fuck!" she yelled, ducking beneath a swinging claw. Diana screamed, wheeling forward as the creature swiped at them, the thick spines of a rock-plated elbow raking ribbons out of her coat and punching into her arm with a wet *crack*. Shaw yelped as the thing batted an elbow in her direction, scrambling back against the wall and rolling desperately out the way. Someone grabbed her – Cale, Diana, she wasn't sure, it didn't matter – and she was hurtling forward again. Hot breath on her back as she pitched toward the tunnel mouth. Henry screaming at them to hurry up, to run. Cale, somewhere behind her, yowling as a bloody claw shredded the back of his leg.

Shaw tumbled out of the tunnel mouth and into the arctic.

Time seemed to stop for a moment as the vast emptiness of the tundra spread wide before her. The sky was not black but a seeping, ink-spattered grey, tumbling waves of moonlight riding the distant horizon like spraying water. Somewhere distant a polar bear bellowed softly; elsewhere, less distant, another mournfully responded. An infinite sea of stars formed a blinking, shifting dome above her, the distant mountains and glaciers crips stripes of black blotting out the sky, not formed of colour but an absence of it; the tundra was endless and terrible, painted grey and swirling. She could not see the snow falling around her but felt it, falling into her hair, into her eyes, filming her vision and pressing her body downward, the air heavy with it, saturated with it. Shaw wheeled around and gaped back at the tunnel mouth, her eyes tracking upward, following the curved pelt of the glacier they had escaped until it plateaued in a blinding stripe of almost-fluorescent white. There was the moon, behind the glacier, an enormous ball of light that bled onto the ice in folding and unfolding stripes of brilliance.

The five of them stood there for a moment, struck helplessly by the cold and the infinite flat desert of white around them. Henry stood doubled over with his hands on his knees, panting hard. His glasses had fallen from his face and his eyes were raw and bloodshot; he was sobbing, she realised, weeping helplessly into the snow. Beside him Megan turned a full circle, hands on her head, gazing out into the arctic. *What now?* Where *now?*

"We have to keep going," Shaw urged. "Come on, all of you, we need to *run.*"

"Where?" Henry said, shaking his head. He looked up. "We don't—"

Goliath erupted from the tunnel mouth and snatched Henry with both hands, wrenching him out of the snow. Henry screamed – Megan lurched forward, shrieking too – kicking and struggling as the enormous creature lifted him into the air. Shaw yelled his name uselessly, Cale lifting his harpoon beside her, his arms shaking so badly that he couldn't hold it steady. "Put him down! Put him the fuck—"

With a wet slopping and a thick, staggered round of cracking, crunching sounds, Goliath ripped Henry's body in two. It took only a moment but that moment seemed to stretch into forever: the moon formed a spectral halo around the titan's stone-plated body as it snapped its muscular arms outward, separating Henry right down the middle. There was an oceanic spray of blood as the man's body split violently in half. The screaming stopped abruptly and the creature discarded his flailing halves like useless cuts of meat, throwing them into the snow and taking a step forward. Blood ran in thick sheets down the beast's chest and it grinned.

"No," Diana moaned, her voice coming at Shaw through tar. "No, no, it's all my fault, we should have stayed, we should have *stayed*…"

"Back up," Shaw said calmly as the beast took another step. "Back up, back up—"

She raised her harpoon and drew a breath. Cale

stood beside her, Diana grabbing Megan and pulling her back. In the snow two hunks of bloody darkness twitched finally, thick pools of black spreading around them. Gluey ropes hung off the creature's fists. It growled softly with every rattle of its chest, the guttural rumbling of its throat punching walls of hot breath into the night. Shaw pressed her finger to the trigger, holding her breath, pinning the tip of the harpoon to the gruesome image of Goliath's face. One—

Two—

A powerful bolt of white smashed into Goliath's side and the beast wheeled back on one foot. Shaw swung the harpoon to follow the thing's movement, swearing as it was beaten back. Preparing to fire again, she froze as another white shape dropped onto the creature's shoulders and it bellowed in annoyance. Slowly, she lowered the harpoon.

"Oh my god…" Diana whispered beside her.

A third polar bear lurched out of the snow, smashing its jaws into Goliath's hip and ripping at the stony flesh, an animalistic half-moan, half-snarl detonating inside its throat. There were four of them, attacking the giant creature from all sides. One bear clung to the thing's back as it swung blindly, digging its teeth into Goliath's throat and ripping out a snapping rope of red-purple elastic cable. Black blood winged the snow as the fourth bear butted its entire body into the backs of the giant's knees, sending it crumpling forward. The pack moved like heavy balls of lightning, snapping and yawing at the creature, working together to drag it onto its knees. As Shaw watched in awe, the creature swung a massive fist into the belly of one of the polar bears, sending it sprawling and bleating into the snow. It staggered onto all fours, shaking itself off before letting loose a deafening roar and pouncing again.

"Come on," Diana said quietly, taking her arm. "We can't stay to watch."

ELEVEN

TERROR AT THE TOP OF THE WORLD

The four of them ran into the endless tundra, leaving the giant and its attackers far behind. Blood dropped into the snow behind them, a zigzagging trail of drops that steamed quietly in the dark.

"We can't run forever!" Megan yelled, heaving herself through the snow. It was impossible to run; her feet sunk eight inches with every step. They weren't running, not really, not at all; they were *wading* away from it. "Are we even heading for base camp? You know what's out there, don't you? Past the ice? The ocean, for fuck's sake!"

Shaw looked back over her shoulder. There was no sign of the thing, not yet, but she had a feeling the polar bears wouldn't be enough to finish it. "We need to kill it," she panted. She'd had the chance, back there, had the harpoon pinned right on it – even when the bear had bowled Goliath out of the way, she'd had the *chance*… why hadn't she taken it? Was it cowardice? Something else?

No, she knew why she hadn't fired. Why she hadn't even *tried* to fire, back in the tunnels.

The harpoons weren't going to work. But there must be something…

"What was that thing with the cross?" Cale asked, reaching the same conclusion a moment before she could find the breath to voice it. His own voice was shaky, fragile, sucked into the wind before it could fully reach her.

"I don't know!" Diana yelled. She glanced at Cale, her eyes wide. Out of breath, she went on: "I think it's old, this thing. Really old. Like, *Biblical* old."

"So what, it's… like, a demon or something?" Megan shouted. "You realise that's *nuts*?"

"I don't think it's a demon," Diana said. The four of them had slowed to walking pace, struggling through the snow. It had become suddenly more shallow and Shaw felt that she could sense the ocean beating at the ice beneath them. Was it thinner here? Christ, what if they fell through? As if they needed one more thing to worry about.

"What, then?" Cale said.

"Does it matter?" Shaw hissed. "Does it matter what it is? If we don't find a way to kill it—"

"Yes," Cale said. "Look, whatever you did with that cross, Diana, it *worked*. Just for a second, but it worked. So whatever you think this thing is—"

"I think it's Behemoth," Diana said quietly.

They had stopped moving now, standing ankle-deep in the snow, the ice shifting beneath them. Shaw cocked an eyebrow. "I'm sorry, you think it's what?"

Diana swallowed. "*Behemoth.* Behemoth and Leviathan were two… beasts, in the Book of Job. Enormous things. More powerful than anything human. Leviathan was a giant of the ocean – I guess a giant serpent, if you go with some illustrations – and Behemoth was this titanic… *thing*, a primeval thing with enormous strength. I think… he was only mentioned once, but his arms were like iron."

"You think that's what this is?" Cale said.

"It was speaking, before. Aramaic. And if it's that old – if it's been *frozen* out here since the days of the Bible…"

"Okay," Megan said, shaking her head as she peered into the dark behind them. She was shivering uncontrollably. "So what can we do?"

"I don't know," Diana said. "The cross worked, but it wasn't enough. We need… I don't know. Silver. Holy water. Sacred blades—"

"Do we have any of that?" Cale said.

"No."

"Well, then we're fucked," Shaw said. "Now we need to run, and if we reach the sea, we need to—"

"It's coming!" Megan yelled, pointing a shaking finger into the tundra.

Diana turned to look.

The thing seemed to have grown – or it was closer than it looked – and its arms and legs were thicker and more gnarled than before. Its shoulders were mountains of rocky spines, its eyes boiling yellow electricity.

The four of them stood, helpless, on the ice, and Behemoth charged toward them.

Megan shrieked as the creature swung an arm into her side, barrelling her into the snow. Before she could turn onto her back something had come down hard on the back of her leg: she heard the enormous *pop* of bone long before she felt it, and by the time the bolt of pain had shot into her hip a thick set of gnarled, bony claws had punched into her back.

"No!" Diana yelled, stumbling helplessly forward as Goliath tightened its fingers inside Megan's back and twisted ripping her spine up and out of her body like a sloppy, stringy carry-handle. Megan's screams were cut violently short as the beast grabbed her head with its free hand and cradled the shelf of her jaw, almost gently. Her eyes landed briefly on Diana's before rolling up into her head, then the creature yanked upward, hard, pulling her skull half off her shoulders. Her neck strained, then seemed to burst, wings of red spraying the snow as the viscera of her windpipe as exposed, stretched, and then snapped. Diana sobbed, clamping a hand over her mouth. The ice shuddered as the titanic creature slammed Megan's limp body down, ploughing her bloody upper half deep into the snow. Diana shook her head, wanting desperately to go forward but knowing it was too late – besides, she couldn't move, couldn't breathe—

"Get back," Cale said calmly, stepping up beside her. He raised the harpoon in both arms, swinging the spear up toward the giant's throat. Before she could do as he'd said, Cale fired, squeezing the trigger and gritting his teeth, tangles of hair caught in his mouth, in his eyes, which flashed with a bright knot of anger as the harpoon kicked back into his shoulder.

The spear sailed out of the barrel, trailing a thick black cable as it launched itself at the giant's face. The creature wheeled around, its own eyes flaring that dreadful flickering canary-yellow. Its face was all stone now, every part of its body; the cracks between the plates were an awful blotchy red like frostbitten skin, but the creature had been turned so horribly inside-out that they couldn't be flesh, not really. Thin runnels of crimson were visible between the spikes and roots twisting across the creature's back.

The harpoon punched into its chest and bounced off, the cable whipping loudly as it ribboned in the air. Cale swore, staggering backward to reel it in; too late. Diana yelled in anguish as the creature reached down, folding its fingers around the spear, and tearing the cable like paper. Cale stumbled as the thick black wire snapped back at him, then threw the harpoon gun itself in a desperate last-ditch attempt. It sailed a mile wide.

The creature roared, a single word in that ancient, Biblical language, bellowing it at the top of its lungs like a war cry. The inside of its mouth was black and wet, the crushed rocks of its teeth stained orange with blood.

Shaw yelled out as she lurched forward, the second harpoon raised. Goliath took a stomping step toward them and Diana reached out to grab Cale's arm, but swiped at empty air. She turned her head to see him staggering away, shaking his head. She turned back to the creature. "Go!" she yelled, and Captain Shaw fired.

The creature stomped its foot in the ice just as the harpoon sunk into its stomach, somehow finding a home between two outcrops of twisted sediment. The ice shuddered again and it roared, grabbing the spear and wrenching it free with a spurt of black. "It's useless!" Shaw yelled. "They're not doing any—"

The two of them screamed as the creature smashed its foot down a third time. The tundra shook as if a meteorite had sailed into the pole and a thin grey crack splintered outward from the beast's toes, widening as it stepped forward again. Diana grabbed desperately for Shaw's hand and pulled her across the crack, the two of them falling into the snow. Goliath launched its knuckles into the ground and the crack yawed open, several smaller crevices widening as chunks of ice billowed into mist in the air.

Shaw yanked back the cable and started jamming

the harpoon back into the gun, looking up frantically as the titan approached. Another pounding footstep boomed across the ice, a web of deep splinters forming immediately around its foot. "Come on," Diana yelled, grabbing Shaw's arm. She looked around desperately, yelling for Cale's help, but he was gone. The fucker had abandoned them, she realised with a sinking feeling in her stomach. He had realised he was more likely to survive if he became the smaller party, and he'd legged it into the snow. Maybe she'd been right about the bastard all along. "*Coward!*" she spat, dragging Shaw to her feet.

Shaw took a bead again and prepared to fire.

The creature lashed out and grabbed her around the stomach, punching the tips of its fingers into her back. Shaw gasped as her ribs cracked loudly, tipping back her head as streaming ribbons of agony engulfed her whole body. Diana grabbed desperately for the older woman's hand but it slipped free as the creature snatched her away. Screaming, Diana lurched forward and took hold of the only thing she could reach, wrapping her fingers around the harpoon in Shaw's right hand. "Hold on!" she yelled.

Goliath was too strong. He wrenched Shaw away – the woman's hand slipped up the shaft of the harpoon, the barbed hook grazing the inside of her wrist and drawing thick beads of blood.

"*NO!*"

The creature dug both hands into her stomach and

ripped it open, Shaw's head lolling back as her chest and guts spilled into the snow. Thick coils of intestine billowed out of her body, followed by a slopping collection of ruptured organs. The creature bore its teeth into her shoulder and shook its head, tearing hunks of meat free and spraying red gobs into the ice.

"No…" Diana whispered, stumbling back, the harpoon in her hands. Utterly helpless, she did the only thing she could: she turned from the creature and ran, tears freezing on her face, into the endless wasteland of the north pole.

TWELVE

BEHEMOTH

Diana seethed as she marched through the snow, frozen air slipping into the ragged tears in her coat. Her back was a slab of brittle ice, her throat burning. Teeth gritted, she ploughed into a whirlwind of white particles, the tundra seeming to shift and sway beneath her. Half-running, she heard the shuddering footsteps behind her and knew the creature had finished with Shaw's carcass.

Cale had left them. That *dick*. Her blood boiled with anger at the man, the terror pumping in her veins battling fury for dominance of her chest. She sped up, moving awkwardly, unable to see the horizon for the batting wings of snow in her face. Blotches of inky black sprayed the back of each snowdrop, the darkening night sky trying to leech through. The fucker had abandoned them, he'd run away when they needed him most – and right when she'd started to really trust him, too – he'd split like the devil as soon as he saw his chance—

Can you blame him?

Diana stumbled, fell onto her knees. Moaning, strings of drool falling from her mouth and freezing onto her chin, she lurched to her feet and waded forward. Her bones were numb and fizzing; even the adrenaline was so slow and subdued that it had stopped reaching her limbs. Her heart pumped weakly, fuelling an empire of cold inside her body. She was going to die.

The ground shook and she wheeled around, lifting the reloaded harpoon. Through an undulating wall of blizzard-wool she saw the blurred silhouette of the beast, shadowy spikes exploding from every joint and corner, its impossible shoulders sprouting wings of rock like curled antlers. It towered above her, twice her height now, fists like boulders; its eyes were headlights in the snow, piercing cones of yellow setting banks of swirling white on fire.

Diana screamed with every ounce of rage in her body as she squeezed the trigger, pumping the harpoon into the electric mist.

The cable snapped taut and the barbed head of the harpoon sunk into something solid. One of those flickering yellow lights blinked out completely and the creature yowled, its vague silhouette growing into something oblique and terrifying as it spread its hands in agony.

Diana yelped as the creature reached up and yanked

the harpoon out of its eye. Something warm splashed her face but she hardly noticed it among the millions of plump, cold drops flying into her eyes. She staggered backward, reeling the cable back toward her, ducking out of range of a swiping paw and turning heel and running and cursing as she fumbled to reload the harpoon. It would never work, she'd just shot the blasted thing in the eye and it was still coming, hardly fazed at all—

What did I teach you?

Her father's voice. "Not fucking now," she whispered, jamming the harpoon into the shaft. The ground shuddered as Goliath lunged after her, a couple dozen feet behind – fifteen, now, twelve – and she turned around to fire again, knowing her only hope in the world was to aim at its remaining eye and blind it. But that first hit had been a fluke, she knew as much, and the world was an endless sea of white, it would be impossible to…

What did I teach you? said the voice again, and she froze.

The creature's silhouette loomed out of the white, single eye glinting in its head like a miniature sun.

"Oh," Diana whispered. She didn't have time. There was no way—

Before she could talk herself out of it, she sunk to her knees, wrapped both hands around the harpoon, and slammed the butt of the harpoon into the ice. There was no way of knowing how thick it was here – could have been two feet, could have been two metres – and she yelled as she brought the harpoon up again, then brought it crashing down. The ice directly beneath her shuddered, though that might have been another of the creature's massive footsteps. Looking up through stiff, frozen tangles of hair and a wall of pure white, she saw nothing but that tiny yellow light, high above her like a distant lighthouse. She roared, smashing the butt of the harpoon down again.

A tiny crack splintered around the harpoon and she moaned into the wind, bringing it crashing down a fourth time. "Come on!" she yelled, using all the strength she had left to smash the thing into the ice again, again – *again.* "*COME ON!*"

The creature roared and she looked up, eyes wide, saw the massive silhouette materialise out of the snow as it lurched forward, swiping its claws at her face—

A ball of white exploded against the side of its head and it blinked, that single burning eye extinguished for a fraction of a second. It turned, distracted, and Diana followed its gaze. Her lungs heaved as she saw a tiny silhouette in the snow, recognising it immediately. Her heart pounded. "Cale!"

The creature turned as another snowball pelted it in the mouth, an expert shot spraying tiny fragments into its teeth. It spat out snow and roared, more irritated than hurt, but for the time being distracted at least. It lunged in Cale's direction and the tiny silhouette ducked, crumpling onto its back in the snow. "I don't know what the hell you're doing," Cale yelled, "but keep at it!"

Diana screamed, punching the harpoon into the ice with more force than she'd imagined she could muster. A couple dozen feet away the beast slammed its fists into the ice either side of Cale's vague shadow, cracking the ground instantly. The ice field shuddered. The tiny web of splinters Diana had created opened a little wider and she took her opportunity, slamming the harpoon into its shaft and firing down into the ice.

The spear seemed to slip into the ice as if it were water. She yanked upward and the barbed tip wrenched chunks of ice free, leaving a tiny furrow between her feet. Elsewhere the creature seemed to have landed a fist; she heard Cale wheeze in pain and a sick, wet *crack* boomed across the tundra. "Nearly there!" she yelled. A tiny narrow tunnel had appeared beneath her, drilling down into the ocean beneath the ice. With every fibre of being, she slammed the harpoon butt into the ground one last time – just as the creature stomped a foot into Cale's back, breaking it and cracking the ice open.

Diana bent over the thole she'd made and looked down into the black water below. Tossing the harpoon away, she folded her hands together and looked up, watching as the creature picked Cale up and slammed him into the ground like a ragdoll. Tears streamed down her face as she started to speak, to pray:

"Lord, Creator of all life, God Almighty, bless this

water, as we use it in faith: forgive our sins, many as they may be, and save us from the power of evil—"

The creature roared, beating its knuckles into Cale's face and breaking bone. It threw the man into the ground and Cale yelled in agony as it stamped its heel on the back of his leg, shattering an already broken limb.

"Cale!" Diana yelled, faltering for a moment. *Salt,* she thought, *I don't have any salt,* and then the ridiculousness of that hit her and she swallowed, nauseous.

"Keep... going—"

She focused, squeezing her eyes shut, plunging one gloved hand into the drillhole she'd formed at her feet. *"Lord God Almighty, bless this water, as we use it in faith – forgive our sins – please, forgive our sins – and save us from all illness, and from... from the power of evil—"*

There was an almighty splintering sound as the creature ploughed all its weight into Cale's spine. The ice beneath them exploded open, a storm of white hunks detonating in the air as they were sucked downward. The plates of ice either side of the crevice sloped upward like wings, then crashed back into each other – Goliath was gone.

For a second, the ice was very still.

Diana staggered to her feet, lunging forward, pelting toward the spot where Cale and the beast had been only moments before. "Cale!" she yelled. "Cale, can you hear—"

She stopped at the edge of the crack, the ice before her split into slurry and ragged hunks. The ocean below seethed, bubbling furiously, boiling: thick black plumes of smoke gathered below her and spread into seeping clouds of popping mini-explosions as they reached the top of the churning pool.

Right below the surface she saw Cale, his body broken, bubbles streaming out of his mouth and joining the others. His arm was bent behind him at an unnatural angle, both legs buckled. His back was arched and stiff, his face a mess of red and purple that hadn't washed off in the water: those were bruises. His chest was savaged, thick trenches carved through his ribs; the flesh at the edges bubbled red. Diana scrambled to her knees and reached forward, preparing to thrust both arms into the water and try and pull him out, then stopped herself.

Slowly, infinitely slowly – had the water subdued his movements to such an impossible degree, or had time itself begun to drag against the skin of the world? – Oliver Cale winked.

Beneath him an enormous black shape was sinking fast, a single flickering yellow light growing smaller and dimmer as enormous reams of red broke off the creature's stony flesh and turned to bloody mist in the water.

Diana watched the two of them sink for what felt like hours, her face warmed by the steam rising off the thrashing surface of the water.

Holy water.

The whole ocean? she wondered. No, she'd been lucky that it had reached this far. Unless…

It didn't matter. She unfolded, somehow managing to rise to her feet, her hands hanging uselessly at her sides. Beneath her the water simmered softly, the bubbles slowing; pools of red clotted on the surface, freezing over already. The yellow light had gone out.

Behemoth was dead.

THIRTEEN

HEADING SOUTH

Diana sobbed as she waded through the snow, pummelled from all sides by thick banks of wind. Snow in her mouth, in her hair, in her eyes. the adrenaline had begun to wear off and now her body was pushed forward by a thick, throbbing swell of survivor's guilt. She didn't know if she was heading for base camp, but she had resigned herself to walking until she reached the ocean, then turning and traversing the coastline until she saw some sign of civilisation.

If she died before that, so be it. They had been sent here to rescue the survivors at the research base; they had failed. There was no escaping the fact that she had let them down. Even survival didn't feel like the small victory that it was: what use was it escaping the beast when she had killed the rest of them?

Goliath – Behemoth, whatever he was – hadn't killed them.

She had.

They would have died anyway, she tried to tell herself. If she hadn't convinced them to leave the base, they would have been picked off, one at a time, until they were all gone. There was no denying that.

But at least it wouldn't have been her fault.

She stumbled, almost falling to her knees in the ice. She knew that if she fell again, she wouldn't get up. That would be enough. She felt faint – black clouds gathered at the edges of her vision – and she realised how thirsty she was, how much her stomach hurt. It had stopped asking for food now and started threatening to eject everything inside her. She felt more uncomfortable than pained, but she knew the pain would return once her senses had ceased their numb tingling. She just had to get warm, get to shelter, to food… she had to pee, badly.

No stopping. Keep going. Keep—

The ice rumbled. Ever-so-faintly, so that she was almost sure she had imagined it. But the slight tremor beneath her feet was enough to make her stop, to make her listen.

She stood there for thirty seconds before it rumbled again.

Louder this time.

"No…" she whispered. He was back. It hadn't been enough. No, oh God, no…

She turned, slowly, gazing back in the direction she had come from. Above the distant mountains, ribbons of beautiful green light pelted each other like waves.

Great streaks of iridescence danced between the softly-swaying bands of colour, knots of blue and aqua glittering with moonlight as they preyed on thick, swelling clumps of emerald.

The ice beneath was still. Still and wide and infinite, stretching for eternity before her.

It rumbled again.

"No," Diana moaned, shaking her head. It couldn't be…

This time the rumbling didn't stop. It grew, intensifying, clarifying—

A mile from where she stood, the ice detonated. The tundra erupted into a shower of bright white, enormous chunks barrelling across the wasteland as something *surged* upward from beneath. Something massive, bigger than Behemoth, bigger than anything she could imagine…

"Oh, no."

The serpent thrust its head up through the ice with a colossal spray of black ocean water, great walls of glassy ice pouring from its mouth as it screamed into the sky. Its neck followed, thick and ribboned with banks of purple and green, every single scale the size of Diana's head – and there were *millions* of them, running in great shining runnels across the great sea-snake's body – its head must have been twice the size of Behemoth's entire body, its eyes round and shining—

The serpent's body thumped onto the ice and

screamed at her, giant fangs burrowing into the crust. A great frill of aquamarine bristled around its throat and it narrowed its eyes. Two or three miles away, another explosion drilled up through the tundra and the tip of the serpent's tail lashed upward, smashing into the sky and lashing the stars out of existence.

"*Leviathan,*" Diana whispered.

The serpent hissed. Its nose was patterned with patches of boiling flesh, raw red meat showing through peeling curls of scaly skin. The holy water had spread farther than she'd realised – deeper, too…

She had woken it.

"Shit," Diana said, and she crumpled to her knees in the snow as Leviathan thrust toward her, its mouth yawing open as black and wide as the mouth of the polar cave she should have died in.

A NOTE FROM THE AUTHOR

Thank you for reading *Empire of Cold*. As an independent author every single person reading my work is so valued and I can't express how much your time means to me. For more of my books, follow me on Instagram @heath_horrorwriter or check out my website derekheathhorror.com where I'll keep you updated on future releases.

I hope you enjoyed! If so, please leave a review on Amazon if you can. I'd love to know what you thought.